Pawsitively
A
Match
Purrfect

I0580798

Unbearably Cute

Unbearably Cute

A PAWSITIVELY PURRFECT MATCH

PEPPER MCGRAW

Contents

P
M
G
Publishing

<h1 style="text-align:center">One</h1>

BYGUL WAS THE top matchmaking cat at Pawsitively Purrfect Matches. That might seem a tad arrogant for him to claim, but since everyone else agreed with him, he was just being truthful and that was all.

Bygul had a number of earthbound cats assigned to him at the moment, all of them needing human companions. These were the matches PPM was known for and Bygul, like all the other working cats of PPM, specialized in these types of matches.

What set Bygul apart from the rest of them, though, was his additional specialization in love matches.

The goddesses hadn't exactly approved in the beginning. They considered love matches to be *their* domain, but when Bygul pointed out that a love match made by the cat of a goddess was really the same as a love match made by the goddess herself, they began to see the possibilities.

Unfortunately, those possibilities included having Bygul train fifty other matchmaking cats to make their own love matches on behalf of the goddesses.

This was when Bygul's purrfectly wonderful job acquired a few additional, not-so-purrfect responsibilities.

Being asked to train others might seem like a compliment at first, but Bygul knew the truth.

It was punishment!

He was being punished for his excellence, which was entirely unfair.

At first, there seemed to be no escaping his fate.

However, after weeks of trying to train unruly cats in the art of romance (and failing miserably), the unexpected happened.

It was a miracle really.

Slowly, one by one, the cats began to lose interest in learning how to make love matches and stopped showing up for classes.

This was excellent news as far as Bygul was concerned. In a matter of weeks, he'd gone from fifty trainees to only three.

Unfortunately, those final three were the most stubborn of the lot and they showed no signs of giving up anytime soon.

That was when he began plotting against them. With the nicest of intentions, of course. He was only trying to save them from a lifetime of failure and disappointment, after all.

Hopefully, the goddesses would notice if the cats made a disastrous match, or if they failed to make one at all, and would release all of them (but most especially Bygul) from this training nightmare.

To get started, all he needed was a suitably impossible matchmaking mission.

Happily, he had the perfect candidate in mind.

Grumpy, unruly, rude, loud, obnoxious, alpha bear shifter *Mason Worcester*.

The bear's personality was bad enough, but add in his penchant for throwing other shifters through windows and doors and off rooftops and over the side of mountains and the results were clear.

Mason Worcester was (and Bygul did not use this word lightly) *unmatchable*.

Which made him the purrfect target.

"YOU WANT TO WHAT?" JEFFERSON EXCLAIMED incredulously.

"Well, you don't have to say it like that." Kate had no idea why her mate was so astonished. It was a perfectly brilliant idea.

"You're mad," Jefferson said, "and I won't be a party to it. It's cruel."

"It's a kitten, not a torture device."

"Exactly. A poor, defenseless kitten you're planning to feed to your psycho brother."

Rude! Kate let a minuscule roar escape and smirked when Jefferson leapt backwards, clearing the span of the office in one leap.

At the same time, her assistant, Nick, jumped, sending his chair flying out from under him and dumping him on the floor. He glared over his shoulder at Kate, but she didn't know why he was so upset.

It's not like he wasn't used to it by now.

If he didn't like it, he shouldn't sit down in the first place. He had a standing desk for a reason, after all.

Besides, that roar had been halfhearted at best. Why, the windows had barely rattled—she glanced through them to the garage below—and the mechanics hadn't even hit the deck this time.

"I tried to stop her, Cleocatra," Jefferson said mournfully.

Kate whirled and glared at him.

He was cradling his black kitten in his arms, stroking her fur and crooning to her in that way he had, the one that made Cleocatra believe she was the center of his world, something that also made her a holy terror when she felt someone else (usually Kate) was attempting to usurp her role as queen of his universe.

Which, to be honest, Kate did quite often, especially

since the way he stroked Cleocatra made Kate imagine all sorts of naughty things involving him stroking her.

"I can't be held responsible for the tragedy to come, Cleocatra," Jefferson said as he slowly stroked his hand down the kitten's back. "I've done my best and now we must all suffer for my failures."

Oh, for heaven's sake. She was surrounded by drama queens. "What are you going on about now?"

Jefferson ignored the question and continued his one-sided conversation with the kitten. "Just remember when the poor kitten gets eaten, or worse, tossed through a window —" he sent a scorching look her way "—it's all Kate's fault."

"My brother would *never*—"

"As someone he's thrown through a window—not once, but twice, mind you—I have to respectfully disagree. *He would.*"

"You were a stranger he'd never met before and you were kissing *me*, his baby sister. What did you expect?"

"Uh, for him to kindly wait until I stopped kissing you and then to introduce himself politely?"

Kate stared at him incredulously. "You do know my brother is an alpha bear, right?"

"So?"

Kate rolled her eyes.

"And while we're on the subject, what about the second time? So maybe he didn't know who I was the first time he launched me through the air, but that second time was pure maliciousness."

Kate turned away so her mate wouldn't see the smirk on her face. "Oh, stop being such a baby. The point is, yes, my brother might toss you around a bit every once in a while—"

"A *bit*?"

"—but he would never hurt a sweet kitten. He adores Cleocatra, you know that."

"I know he's trying to steal her from me," Jefferson growled, "but for what reason I have no idea. What would a psycho–bear want with a tiny kitten anyway? Nothing good, that's for sure."

"Oh, for heaven's sake. Melodramatic much?"

"All I'm saying is maybe you should consider a python or an alligator or — what am I saying? Your psycho brother's the top of every food chain, so really it's better if you choose an entirely different gift for him. No pets for the apex predator!"

Kate snickered. "It's not like I'm suggesting we give him Cleocatra."

The kitten, who was now perched on Jefferson's shoulder, turned her entire body so that she was facing Kate and bared her fangs.

Little monster!

Every time Kate thought she'd finally won the kitten over, Cleocatra went out of her way to prove that she only tolerated Kate and could, in fact, shred her to ribbons at any moment.

Kate lifted her lip, planning to unleash just one of her

fangs when she caught sight of the amused look on Jefferson's face and scowled instead.

He should be defending his mate's honor instead of finding amusement in the antics of a tiny little beast who was constantly riling up her bear.

"Anyway," Kate growled, glaring at the two of them, "I'm going to the rescue organization and I'm choosing a kitten for my brother. Are you coming along or not?"

"Not," Jefferson said decisively, as he turned and strode toward the office door. "Even if I didn't have a garage full of repairs, I still would have nothing to do with this plan to feed a defenseless kitten to that psychotic bear."

"My brother isn't—"

The door slammed, cutting off her protest.

"Dude," Nick said. "You're brother's *so* psychotic."

Kate snickered. "Stop it. He is not."

"Okay, fine. He's out of control, overbearing, outrageously rude... come on, help me out here."

"I mean, all of that is true, but that doesn't make him psychotic."

"No, but throwing people off a cliff kind of does."

"He only ever did that once and it was totally justifiable. Assuming it even happened. I maintain the possibility of his innocence."

Nick raised an eyebrow.

"Besides, Dorian forgave him."

"Eventually. After he woke from that coma. How long did it take him again? A year?"

"Oh, don't exaggerate. It was only ten months."

"What were they fighting about again? Raisinets? Junior Mints?"

"Milk Duds. The last box. I mean, who could blame him? He was a hungry bear. Everyone knows you don't get between a bear and his food."

"But the food was *Dorian's*. And let's not forget that Dorian's a bear too."

"Sure, but Dorian wasn't the *alpha* bear."

"Neither was Mason. At least, not then."

"Are you insinuating that it wasn't obvious my brother was an alpha bear from the moment he let out his first roar?"

Nick made a face. "Okay, fine. Doesn't make it any less psychotic."

"He was five!"

Nick snickered. "And Dorian, how old was he again?"

"Sixteen!"

"Yeah. You do realize none of this is proving him any less psychotic. What kind of five-year old attacks a sixteen year old and wins?"

Kate let out a huff of exasperation. "Isn't it obvious? An alpha bear, of course."

Nick let out a snort.

"Besides, Mason's gained a lot of—okay, *some* control —since then. After all, he hasn't tossed anyone off a mountain since. Not even when they make him really mad."

"No, he just tosses them through windows and on one

memorable occasion, from The Worcester Group's rooftop."

"That employee was embezzling funds. He's lucky Mason didn't kill him."

Nick nodded. "Yeah, I guess that is pretty indicative that he's gained *some* control. You shouldn't tell Jefferson that though."

Kate grinned. "Of course not. It's entirely too much fun torturing him. Especially after that second launching."

"You can tell me all about it on our way to the animal shelter."

"WHAT DO YOU MEAN I CAN'T JUST ADOPT A kitten?" A woman's irate voice rang through the quiet of the shelter, breaking Isana's train of thought and making her lose track of the numbers she was currently crunching as she attempted to balance the shelter's accounts, a task she'd put off until the very last minute, like she always did.

"You have way more kittens than you need around here. Surely you can spare a few."

Isana rolled her eyes.

Great.

Yet another human convinced the entire animal kingdom had been set on this earth for their convenience.

Isana couldn't hear the volunteer's response, but she imagined it was apologetic, yet firm.

Not that it seemed to matter.

"Look, I filled out the application like you asked. Now I'd like to choose a kitten and get on with my day."

Isana heaved a sigh.

Clearly she wouldn't be finishing the accounts until this woman had either been satisfied or sent away.

Closing her laptop, Isana stood and walked out of her office and down a short hall into their reception area, where her volunteer Sarah was looking a bit agitated as she faced off with—

Isana dragged in a deep breath.

Oh, great.

Not a human after all.

"Can I help you?" Isana moved behind the counter and nodded to Sarah, who looked terribly relieved as she scurried away.

As anyone would be, facing off against a grizzly.

Isana scowled at the woman. "Was it really necessary to intimidate poor Sarah? She's not a bear, you know."

The woman looked surprised. "I'm not intimidating." She whirled to face the wolf at her side. "Right, Nick?"

The wolf let out an odd choking sound, whirled and raced toward the outer door. He flung it open and disappeared outside.

He wasn't quite fast enough though, for the door hadn't quite closed when they heard his burst of hysterical laughter.

The woman rolled her eyes. "Wolves. So dramatic, am I right?"

She *was* right, but Isana wasn't sure she really wanted to bond with a grizzly, so she didn't reply.

"Right. Sorry. I'm Kate and I'm here to adopt a kitten for my brother. I've filled out the application." She shoved it across the counter toward Isana.

Isana picked up the paper, but didn't look at it. "I'm surprised your brother wants a cat and not a dog. I can recommend some dog rescues if he'd prefer that."

Kate looked confused. "Why would he want a dog?"

"Well, I just figured since he's a wolf—"

"Oh, goodness no. We're bears!"

"Oh, I'm terribly sorry. I thought he was a wolf." Isana waved a hand toward the front door, feeling a bit ashamed that she'd stereotyped the shifter based purely on scent, something she was always judging others for doing.

"Nick?" Kate snickered. "He's not my brother. He's my assistant and just came along to help pick out the kitten." She threw a scowl over her shoulder. "Lot of help he is right now, running away like that." She glanced back at Isana. "How can he help choose the perfect kitten for Mason if he isn't even in here to meet them?"

Isana shook her head. "I'm sorry. I'm not sure I understand. Is your brother here?"

"Oh, no. It's a surprise. For Christmas, you know."

Isana couldn't even express the horror she felt at the thought. "Absolutely not."

"Excuse me?"

"Do you have any idea how many cats and dogs and rabbits and other animals get adopted for birthdays and holidays and *surprises*—" Isana waved her arms in agitation, "only to be surrendered months later back to the same shelters they were adopted from, or even worse, are simply thrown outside and abandoned to the wild?" She glared at Kate. "Do you?"

"Well, no, but I assure you, Mason will be thrilled. He's fallen in love with my mate's kitten, you see, and well, Jefferson's rather attached to Cleocatra and isn't willing to give her away, so we're stuck with her, but Mason's awfully lonely, now that I'm not around as much and so I thought a kitten would be a lovely surprise for him."

"Kittens are not surprises!" Isana had no idea why people couldn't seem to grasp this very simple concept. "They're living beings and they need cared for every day for the rest of their lives. That isn't a surprise. That's a responsibility! It's a lifelong commitment. It's not to be taken lightly."

"Obviously, and I assure you, Mason would take the responsibility very seriously."

"He's a *bear*, isn't he?"

"What?"

"A *bear*. Clumsy, plodding, often completely out of control, irrational *bears.*"

Kate looked confused. "I'm sorry, but aren't *you* a bear?"

Isana jerked back in offense. "I most certainly am *not!*"

Kate raised an eyebrow, leaned across the counter toward Isana and inhaled deeply. "Well, you sure smell like a bear."

"I'm not a bear!"

"If you say so. Anyway, to get back to the point, I'd like to choose a kitten now."

"No kittens!" Isana bellowed.

"Well, that's quite rude. The other gal said you had many kittens."

"We do! We have kittens we'll happily adopt to people who are not giving them as *gifts* or *surprises.* We also have kittens for people who are not *bears!*"

"That seems rather harsh. I mean, I suppose I understand your anti-gift, anti-surprise stance. But your anti-bear attitude seems a bit much."

"What happens if your brother shifts into his bear form and then accidentally steps on the kitten?"

"Unlikely."

"Let me put it this way. What if he goes into a boar rage at someone who irritates him and accidentally stamps on the kitten while raging about?"

Kate seemed to think about that for a moment, then said, "He only goes into rages at work—people tend to annoy him there—so I'll just make The Worcester Group off-limits for cats."

Isana inhaled so quickly and deeply she went a bit lightheaded.

At that moment, Nick came slamming back through the front door. "Are we ready to choose some kittens yet?"

"No!" Isana stormed around the counter, planted her palms on the grizzly's chest and shoved. "Absolutely no gifts!" She shoved again and this time, Kate actually moved. "No surprises!" Shove. "No bears!" Shove. "And absolutely, under no circumstances, will we ever allow Mason Worcester of The Worcester Group to adopt one of our precious kittens!" She shoved one last time and Kate skidded back into the front door.

"Um." Nick sent a wide-eyed look between Isana and Kate.

"Get out!" Isana yelled.

Kate sighed, gave her a sad look, then turned and walked out.

Nick hesitated, then said, though it sounded more like a question, "I'm sorry?" and followed her out.

Two

"T*HAT'S* THE TARGET?" Tivali demanded. She was pacing back and forth on the conference table—at the far end from the bear, of course.

"He *can't* be the target," Soraya wailed from where she was cowering under the conference table. She'd darted under there the second the bear had lost his temper.

"Bygul, please tell us you're joking," Muezza said.

"What's the matter with you guys?" Bygul asked. "You've been begging for weeks that I give you your own target to match and now that I have, you're complaining? I've been making matches like these all by myself for years. Surely you three can manage one measly love match."

"There's nothing measly about him," Soraya exclaimed. "He's absolutely ginormous."

"Not to mention terrifying," Tivali said. "I can't imagine a single cat ever falling in love with him, let alone an actual human being."

"This isn't right," Muezza said. "Admit it. You've saddled us with an unmatchable."

Bygul growled low in his throat. He couldn't believe Muezza had already figured it out! No matter though. Bygul was an expert at misdirection. "There's no such thing as an unmatchable," he informed them in a lofty tone. "There may be difficult matches, but that doesn't mean impossible ones. Sure, some matches might take a bit longer to complete, but who cares? All that means is those targets will cherish their match all the more for how long they had to wait for it."

"I had no idea you were so optimistic, Bygul," Tivali said.

"Not to mention romantic," Muezza muttered with a suspicious scowl. He clearly wasn't convinced.

"Seriously?" Bygul infused as much astonishment as he could into that one word. "I've outmatched every matchmaker in the system. I couldn't possibly have matched that many cats with their human companions and that many humans with their love matches if I weren't both optimistic *and* romantic."

"He's got a point," Soraya said.

"Of course, I do. Now get to work. Because everyone deserves a faithful cat companion *and* a true love match."

MASON WAS ABOUT TWO SECONDS AWAY FROM A full-on boar rage.

He was surrounded by idiots and if there was one thing Mason abhorred over all else, it was stupidity.

"Get out!" He roared, slamming his fists down on the conference table.

Despite himself, he was once again impressed at the workmanship that kept the table from buckling beneath the force of his rage.

Mason's sister, Kate, liked to point out that the table wasn't just bear-proof or even grizzly-proof, but that it was Mason-Worcester-proof.

He missed Kate.

He hadn't realized how much she did to keep him sane throughout the work day until she moved her office to an entirely different town.

He blamed that damn cat, Jefferson Hewitt.

Mason was sure he could have convinced her to come back eventually, but then she'd found her mate and that was that.

Damn cat.

He was glaring at the table, contemplating going on a hunt when his phone buzzed.

All of his executives had fled the room when he roared at them, but he could still hunt them down.

He'd drag the wolves to the ground floor and toss them through the windows there.

The bears, though, those he'd drag to the roof.

Okay, no, not the roof.

That was reserved for thieves and true incompetence.

This time, he'd drag them to the seventh floor.

Or maybe the eighth.

But then his phone buzzed and it was almost like old times.

His sister, Kate, saving both the wolves *and* the bears from his wrath with a single text.

I need you to meet me at this address.

Mason stabbed his phone and scowled at the map that popped up, showing exactly where that address was.

What the hell? *That's not in Worcester Falls.*

No answer.

It's not in Greensboro either.

Still no answer.

Kate. Why am I meeting you in freaking Pleasantville? Mason avoided that town like the plague. Full of humans and—well—humans, they just didn't understand a bear's temperament. Or appetite.

He waited a moment, but when it became evident she wasn't going to answer, he let out a loud huff of exasperation and shoved away from the table.

He stormed out the door of the conference room and

strode through the office, growling at anyone who even looked like they might approach him.

Within seconds, every shifter on the floor was somewhere else.

He let out a grunt of satisfaction.

It was good to be alpha bear.

Fifteen minutes later, he was leaving Worcester Falls, something that had been occurring with increasing regularity lately.

Ever since Kate mated that damn panther, Mason had found himself spending an inordinate amount of time in Greensboro, the shifter town to the west.

Though he'd never admit it to the panther, Mason actually liked the town, though it was no Worcester Falls, which despite the sheer number of wolves living there, was mostly still considered bear territory.

Today, though, Mason was not headed toward Greensboro, where Kate and the panther lived. Instead, he was headed east, straight into Pleasantville.

The only good thing Mason could say about this development was that at least he didn't live there and could escape any time he wanted.

When he first pulled into the parking lot, he was sure he had the wrong address, but a quick check showed he was in the right place.

Mason climbed out of his truck, slammed the door behind him and stared at the monstrosity in front of him.

The building looked as if it had been built in stages, with

different sections added on over the years. Nothing really matched anything else.

The left side of the building was short and squat and had a flat roof. It was also painted purple.

The right side of the building towered over the left and center sections. It was completely circular in shape and had an actual dome for a roof. It would have reminded Mason of a castle tower except for one thing. The entire section, *including the dome,* was painted a brilliant orange.

Between those two sections stood a third section that by itself might have been considered normal. The front wall projected forward beyond the other two sections and was painted a soft cream color. It also boasted a large entrance with a number of windows that looked out onto the parking lot.

Mason imagined this section had been built to try to mesh together the other two, but instead served as a dividing line between bizarre and more bizarre.

"Humans," Mason muttered. You really just couldn't understand them at all.

"Finally!"

Mason grinned at Kate as she stormed across the parking lot toward him.

"It took you long enough."

Mason slung an arm around her and dragged her close for a quick hug.

The moment she started to pull away, he tightened his arms, transforming their casual hug into a full-on bear one.

Kate, of course, immediately began flailing her arms about and struggling to get loose.

Ignoring her struggles, Mason rocked her from side to side and hollered, "Aw, my wee baby sister, how I've missed you so. It's been ages since you last graced me with your presence."

"You idiot," Kate growled, even as she tried desperately, yet futilely, to escape his embrace. "We had dinner two nights ago. Let me loose, you neanderthal!"

Snickers caught Mason's attention and he glanced up to see Nick was standing just a few feet away, grinning like a loon.

"Ah, Nick, good to see you too!" Mason cried out jovially as he moved across the parking lot, dragging his sister with him, maneuvering her just enough so that her face was now smushed into his armpit. He held out his hand and Nick grasped it in his, shaking it with a grin.

"Mason!" Kate howled as she slammed a fist into his gut.

He let out a grunt of both pain and pride—after all, he was the one who'd taught her that move.

"All right, all right, sister mine." He let her loose and grinned as she staggered away, coughing and waving her arms about.

"Grizzly musk," she groaned. "I've been asphyxiated by my own brother's stench."

"Oh, please," Mason said. "If that were the case, you wouldn't be able to talk."

"That'd be the day," Nick said.

"You know, she's always been terribly melodramatic," Mason confided. "Ever since she was a wee little girl."

Nick snickered while Kate just rolled her eyes.

"Now, tell me what we're doing *here*, in front of this odd–looking building, Kate." Mason faced the front entrance and for the first time, noticed the sign. "A cat rescue?" He whirled toward Kate. "Do you need help dragging the panther inside?"

Nick let out a hoot of laughter.

Kate grinned. "Not those kinds of cats. Domesticated ones. Cats and Kittens. Like Cleocatra."

"Hold on a minute. Are you planning to adopt another kitten? Don't you think Cleo might get a bit—"

"Psycho if we bring another cat into the house?" Kate asked dryly. "Yeah, she barely tolerates me as it is. We're here to adopt a kitten for you."

"For me?" Mason was stunned. He'd been so focused on trying to convince Jefferson to let him borrow Cleocatra, it hadn't even occurred to him that he could just get his own kitten. One who would adore him and follow him everywhere and ignore that pesky panther whenever he came around. "This is a great idea!"

"Yeah, well, don't get too excited," Kate said. "We've run into a bit of an issue."

"What kind of issue? Are they all out of kittens?"

"Thankfully, no. However, I made the mistake of mentioning this was going to be your Christmas present to the woman in charge of approving applications and apparently she's a tiny bit anti-gifts."

"Not to mention anti-bear," Nick muttered.

"Who could possibly hate gifts? That doesn't even make sense," Mason said. "This woman must be—wait. Did you say anti-bear?"

Kate grimaced. "Yeah, she's not our biggest fan so now she's holding all the kittens hostage."

"That's just rude!"

"Tell me about it," Kate said. "So we're counting on you to change her mind."

"She is anyway," Nick said. "I'm just along for the ride. And the entertainment value."

"She really said no just because we're bears?"

"Yep," Kate said.

"Unbelievable." The absolute gall of the woman.

Who did she think she was, trying to keep him from adopting his very own sweet, baby kitten?

Why, he could buy this entire building right out from under her, and all the kittens with it, if he wanted.

Not that he had any desire to own such a monstrosity, but just the fact that he could do it should be enough to drag her in line. And if it wasn't, well—

"Let's go. I'm about to steal me some kittens."

Isana had just gotten back into her paperwork when she heard Sarah let out a high-pitched squeak followed by a man speaking in an extraordinarily loud, booming voice.

"I'm here to adopt some kittens. Where do you keep them? Here?"

"Oh, no, you can't—"

"No? How about down here?"

"Wait, you—"

"Still no? Oh, I've got it. Through here, is it? Perfect. Come along, Kate."

"Wait!"

Isana had already been heading to the reception area from the moment she heard his voice, but when she heard him say the name, Kate, she broke into a run.

She skidded into the reception area just in time to see the back of a very large man disappear through the door that led to their veterinary clinic.

"I tried to stop him, Isana," Sarah cried. "But he was determined."

"It's all right, Sarah." Isana glared at Kate, who had opted not to follow the man Isana assumed was her brother, and was instead leaning against their reception counter, grinning. "I know exactly who's to blame." She transferred her glare to the wolf, who was chuckling at Kate's side.

He sobered under her glare. "Hey, don't look at me. I'm too smart to get between a grizzly and his objective, whatever that might be."

"Great." The only reason Isana wasn't chasing after the idiotic bear was because there were no cats in the clinic at the moment. "I suppose your brother's lumbering around the clinic, searching for invisible kittens."

"Oh." Kate looked disappointed. "We thought that was where your cat rooms were." She narrowed her eyes at Sarah. "Did you deliberately look toward that door, just to mislead us?"

A quick glance toward Sarah told Isana that yes, she'd done exactly that. "I'm very impressed, Sarah. Good job."

Sarah sent her a shy smile, one that disappeared when they heard the sound of footsteps approaching.

Loud footsteps. Almost like a stampede really.

Sarah edged away from the door leading into the clinic as the sound of barking reached their ears.

Tarnation! She'd forgotten about the dogs. They didn't usually have dogs at the cat rescue, but a rescue two towns over had desperately needed the space, so Isana had offered up the kennels at the back of the clinic.

The dog rescue sent people over to care for the dogs and some of her volunteers had chipped in as well, but Isana herself hadn't really had any interactions with the dogs. Mostly because dogs didn't really like her.

At all.

So she'd forgotten all about them.

Until now.

When a man came bursting through the door from the clinic, a wild look on his face. "Lion!" He whirled around to face the door he'd just come out of. "Killer lion!" The last word ended in a shriek when a huge furry creature barreled into him and knocked him to the floor.

Isana wasn't certain which rescue was currently sitting on Mason Worcester's chest and attempting to lick him to death, but she did know it wasn't a lion.

"Get it off me! Get it off me!"

Isana rolled her eyes. From the amount of shrieking and flailing, you'd think it really was a lion on his chest.

Isana waited for the bear's sister or for the wolf to help him, but neither seemed inclined at all.

In fact, they were entirely too busy rolling on the floor, laughing hysterically to be bothered with Mason Worcester's panic.

Isana raised an eyebrow at Sarah, but she simply shook her head and stepped back.

Great. No help there.

"For goodness' sake!" Isana exclaimed. "Are you a bear or a bunny rabbit?"

Nick and Kate, who were finally showing signs of sobering up, lost it again. Hanging onto each other, they laughed and laughed.

Rolling her eyes, Isana stalked over to the bear and stood over him, hands on hips, glaring.

He'd stopped shrieking and was now simply lying there, submissive to the giant, shaggy *thing* lying on top of him.

Isana circled around to try and find the thing's head. Ah. There it was. Shaggy fur spilled into its eyes, but that didn't seem to stop it from being able to see as it happily licked every inch of the bear's skin that it could reach.

"I'm not sure if you're aware, Mason Worcester," Isana said. "But *that* is not a lion."

The bear lifted his arm a little to peek out at Isana. "Are you sure?"

"Most definitely. In fact, it's not a cat at all."

Fresh giggling came from where Kate and Nick stood.

"Well, what is it then?" The bear demanded.

Isana grinned. "It's a dog."

And that set the rest of them off again.

From there it took some time to sort things out, getting the dog off the bear, tracking down how the dog had gotten out in the first place (it was the bear's fault, he'd opened the dog's kennel, hoping to find some kittens) and getting the dog back where it belonged.

"I'm adopting that dog," Kate announced.

"Don't be ridiculous!" Mason snapped. "Cleocatra would have a fit. And that dog's a menace."

"Oh, I'm not adopting it for *me*. I'm giving it to Maggie for Christmas."

Isana whirled around and glared at Kate. "Have you learned nothing? What did I say about animals for gifts?"

"But Maggie would adore him and I know it sounds kind of crazy, but I think Genghis Khat and that dog are a match made in heaven."

Mason rolled his eyes. "Forget about the dog. Where are my kittens?"

"There are no kittens available for adoption by bears," Isana said firmly.

"Well, why not?" Mason demanded. "You're a bear!"

"*I am not a bear!*" Isana shrieked. "Now get out!"

"But what about the dog?" Kate asked. "I want to adopt the dog."

"Out!"

Three

"THAT DIDN'T GO well at all," Soraya said, staring at the door through which Kate, Mason and Nick had just been ejected. "Are you sure we can't just pick a kitten from one of our case loads?"

"I told you. I've done my research," Tivali said. "The bear never leaves Worcester Falls. He works, he eats, he goes home, he works some more. He may be the CEO of The Worcester Group, but he's the biggest homebody I've ever seen. If someone has to travel, Kate does it, or one of the other executives."

"What's your point?" Muezza asked.

"My point is the bear's never met his mate, which probably means she doesn't live *or* work in Worcester Falls."

"Oooh, and now he's at the cat rescue in Pleasantville," Soraya said excitedly.

"Exactly." Tivali gave her tail a tiny, yet triumphant swish. "If we had just given him one of our kittens, he'd be back in Worcester Falls right now and not interacting with the two mate candidates we found for him."

"What candidates?" Muezza and Soraya chorused.

"Weren't you paying attention? The two women, Isana and Sarah. They're both definite possibilities."

"Sarah was terrified of the bear and Isana hated him," Muezza pointed out.

"Minor details," Tivali said.

"THAT DIDN'T GO WELL AT ALL," KATE SAID AFTER Isana firmly ejected them from the cat rescue.

"What kind of animal do you think she is?" Mason asked.

"She's a dog, dude," Nick said. "I thought we already established that."

"That doesn't make any sense. She smells like a bear."

"Wait. Who are we talking about?" Kate asked.

"The woman." Mason had been speechless the first time he'd seen her standing above him. Her hair was the purest shade of white he'd ever seen and her bright, green eyes had mesmerized him. Then there was the mystery of her animal. So intriguing.

"What about her?" Kate asked.

"She smells like a bear, but says she isn't one. How can that be? What kind of animal smells like a bear, but isn't a bear?"

Kate shook her head. "I have no idea and I really don't care. We need a plan of action."

"What kind of plan?" Nick asked.

"A plan to adopt a dog."

"But I don't want a dog," Mason said. "I want a kitten."

"Okay, fine. We need a plan to adopt a dog *and* a kitten."

"I don't want just *any* kitten. I need to meet them to make sure they won't be scared of my bear."

Nick snickered. "Dude, you went belly up for a dog. I'm pretty sure no self-respecting kitten will ever fear you again."

Mason lunged for Nick, who let out a high-pitched squeal and backpedalled fiercely. "It was just a joke. Calm down!"

Mason bared his fangs at the wolf. "Yeah, that's what I thought."

"We need to get back to the garage, Nick. We've got some planning to do."

"Yeah, you guys go on ahead. I'm going to hang out a while longer, see if I can charm the bear-not-bear into letting me meet a kitten or two."

Kate rolled her eyes. "Right. Well, good luck with that." As she and Nick walked away, she muttered to him, "We're doomed."

"I heard that!" Mason shouted after them.

Kate just laughed, climbed into her car, waited for Nick to get settled, then drove out of the lot with a tap of the horn.

Finally.

Mason turned and studied the building.

He'd already checked out the rectangular section.

It didn't have much to see.

Offices and some medical rooms, plus some storage spaces and some kennels at the back that had been unexpectedly filled with dogs.

Which made no sense at all since the building was labeled "Cat Rescue."

Of course, he'd assumed the giant, golden beast was a lion. It had more fur than any creature he'd ever seen, except for maybe Bigfoot, and had lunged at him like a predator going after its next meal.

Of course, he'd run away. What rational human being wouldn't run when faced with a hungry predator?

Okay, sure, Mason was a predator too, but his bear had apparently been sleeping on the job when the lion-not-lion broke free, which now that he thought about it, was probably a big freaking clue that the lion was a fake.

Mason scowled. That lion-not-lion had completely freaked him out. *Him. A bear.* He was so ashamed.

Not ashamed enough to give up though.

He studied the building some more.

The clinic was on the left and that was definitely a cat-free zone. The reception area was in the middle and he hadn't seen any cats in there either. So that left the circular tower-like segment to the right.

Excellent.

This time he wasn't going to bother with doors.

ISANA GAVE UP ON THE PAPERWORK WHEN IT became clear she wasn't going to be able to concentrate.

All she could think about was that damn bear.

That huge, growly, demanding, sexy bear.

His scent had wrapped around her when she'd leaned over to drag the dog away and it had taken all of her control to restrain her fox.

Now the vixen was sulking because Isana had kicked out a potential mate, to which Isana reacted with nothing short of horror.

The gods couldn't possibly be so harsh and cruel as to send yet another bear into Isana's life, now could they?

Based on the vixen's state of mind, Isana was afraid they most definitely could.

With a soft growl of annoyance, she shut down her laptop and packed up.

Sarah had left about thirty minutes before, having

completed one final round to make sure all the animals were safe and happy for the night.

Though Isana knew she could trust Sarah's report that all was well, she also never locked up without saying goodbye to each of their rescues one final time.

Though not the dogs, of course.

Visiting them would only rile them up.

She'd just set her bag down on the counter in the reception area when a crash from the cat side of the rescue made her jump.

She lunged across the reception area and flung open the door that led to the cats' quarters.

She loved this area of the rescue center the most.

Because of the cats, of course, but also because it was a truly unique bit of architectural genius.

The lower level of the tower was a giant playroom for cats, with an actual real tree growing at its center.

Around the perimeter of the room was a circular walkway that twined around and around leading higher and higher to the dome at the top. All along the walkway were cat kennels. Each individual kennel could be closed off if that cat needed to be quarantined, but could also be opened so that the cat had free range of several kennels, of an entire floor of kennels or even of the entire complex.

It was truly genius.

But what caught Isana's attention this time wasn't the brilliance of the architecture or even the kennel system that had been built to resemble a fox's intricate den of tunnels.

Instead, it was the giant bear sitting in the middle of the floor, legs forming a triangle that three of her favorite kittens were leaping in and out of.

"Seriously?"

Mason sent her a huge grin. "They're adorable. I think I'm in love."

The tiny colorpoint climbed onto his ankle and started attacking one of his shoelaces.

The two ginger kittens jumped into the bowl his legs had formed and rolled around, wrestling each other.

"How did you get in?"

He shrugged and kept his attention on the kittens, lifting one of the gingers up to his face so he could nuzzle its nose before setting him down and picking up his brother. "I've decided I'm going to adopt all three of them."

Isana's heart clutched. This was the hope for every bonded set of kittens and cats she accepted into the rescue, that they might be adopted together, so that their bond was never broken.

But to a bear? And not just any bear, but a grizzly. And not just any grizzly, but a *Worcester* grizzly. And for that matter, not just any Worcester grizzly, but the *alpha* himself.

It was enough to make her lightheaded.

"There's a process for adoption. You can't just come and decide you're taking three of our kittens and walk out the door with them."

"I don't see why not."

"Because we have to make sure you're the right fit, that

the kittens will bond with you, that you have the right setup at your house, that they'll be safe and loved and happy there."

Mason slowly raised his head and stared at her. "I have more money than I could spend in thirteen lifetimes. If there's something missing at my house that they need, I'll get it. As for bonding—" He looked back down.

The colorpoint had given up on the laces and was now sleeping on his ankle, her four legs wrapped around him securely. The two gingers had stopped wrestling and were now curled up in the curve of one of his knees, also sleeping. The sound of their purring filled the space between Isana and Mason.

Isana rolled her eyes. "There's more to being a pet owner than a few moments of play time."

Mason scowled. "Like what?"

"Like cleaning their litter boxes, feeding them, taking them to the vet for their shots and when they're sick—"

"That's what I have employees for."

"And what if The Worcester Group goes bankrupt tomorrow?"

Mason let out a scoffing sound. "*My* Worcester Group?"

"The point is life is unpredictable and if you're not fully prepared for everything taking care of these kittens entails, you're not getting them."

Mason let out a loud sigh of exasperation. "Fine. What do I need to do to prove I'm worthy of these kittens?"

Isana thought that question right there went a long way

toward proving it, not that she'd ever admit it, and she was charmed in spite of herself. Still, she wasn't one to turn down a brilliant opportunity like this one.

MASON HAD NO IDEA HOW HE'D MANAGED TO GET himself into this situation. All he'd wanted was to adopt one tiny kitten—okay, three tiny kittens—but it shouldn't be that difficult.

Fill out some adoption paperwork, pay the damn fee, leave with the kittens.

But that is not what happened.

He was beginning to think this Isana woman was the devil herself.

Surely only the Dark One could convince him, Mason Worcester, alpha bear of the grizzly Worcesters and CEO of The Worcester Group, to *volunteer* for a cat rescue.

Even worse than volunteering were the tasks involved.

If it was just playing with kittens and cats, he'd have no problem at all with volunteering. He might even make it a permanent gig.

But no. That was *not* all that was involved.

There were the sick kitties who needed medicine, which was a bit like attempting to control the wind.

There was one cat in particular, a huge monster named

Reaper (a more appropriate name Mason couldn't imagine) who wielded his claws much like Mason imagined the Grim Reaper did his scythe.

Unfortunately, Reaper was not a cooperative cat when it came time to give him his medicine, which came in liquid form.

"It's the easiest method of getting medicine down his throat," Isana informed Mason.

He firmly believed she was feeding him a line with that one because there was nothing easy about this shit.

He had Reaper wrapped in a towel, syringe ready to pour the medicine down his throat, and then everything went to hell.

His first attempt ended with a giant scratch across his nose and cheek and don't ask him how the demon cat managed to get his paws free while wrapped in a towel. Clearly, Reaper had ninja powers.

After chasing the cat around the damn room and finally getting him wrapped in the towel again, his second attempt ended with a bunch of medicine coating Reaper's fur instead of in his mouth. Damn cat moved his head at the last minute and all that medicine went to waste.

By the time Mason had caught the cat again and successfully delivered the medicine, he was exhausted.

The cat, on the other hand, was full of energetic fury.

Reaper stalked away and proceeded to ignore Mason for the next hour.

This shouldn't bother Mason as he had many other things to do in that hour, like clean out disgusting litter boxes (how had he gotten into this situation again?) but somehow in the battle between cat and bear, Mason had decided he actually liked Reaper.

Maybe he'd adopt him too. The cat could be a big brother to the kittens, help Mason watch out for them.

When he mentioned this to Isana, she looked horrified. "I'm sorry, now you want to adopt Reaper too? You do know Reaper's a crotchety old man who will probably make you miserable for the rest of his natural life."

Mason shrugged. "That's kind of why I like him."

"Hmmm."

By the time Mason was done cleaning kennels and litter boxes and had fed all the cats (forty-three in all!) he was completely done in.

This job was more exhausting than heading a multi-billion dollar real estate corporation, which was saying an awful lot.

Mason trudged out of the cat wing into the reception area, where Sarah was shutting things down for the evening.

"All finished?" She asked cheerfully.

Mason let out a grunt. "Where's Isana?"

"I'm right here," Isana walked into the room from a hallway at the back of the building. "Sarah, everything good on the dog side?"

"Yes, the volunteers from the dog rescue just left. They

also gave us a stack of their applications, said they trusted us to process them if anyone wanted a dog. They've got their hands full what with taking in all those dogs from the fighting rings and that hoarder's house."

Isana groaned. "Fine. No one's going to come here for a dog though. I mean, it clearly says Cat Rescue on the door."

"You never know. I pass out dog rescue information all the time. This way we can actually show them some available dogs."

"I suppose." Isana sighed. "But we've got forty-three cats we need to find homes for. Forty-three! I'll never understand why people don't just get their animals fixed."

"Well, good news," Mason said heartily. "You'll only have thirty-nine once I'm out of here." He rubbed his hands together. "Now, what do you need me to fill out so that I can take my wee cats home?"

"He really thought that was going to work," Soraya observed.

"For supposedly running an entire corporation, the man isn't that smart," Tivali said.

"Yeah," Muezza agreed. "Even I knew one afternoon of volunteering wasn't going to convince Isana of anything."

Tivali winced as Mason stormed out of the rescue

center, waving his arms and shouting about devil women. "He's never going to win a mate with that kind of attitude."

Mason paced in the parking lot a few moments, then turned and stormed back toward the building.

He flung open the door and shouted inside, "I'll be back tomorrow after work. I'm not giving up! Those cats are mine." He stormed away.

"Oh, that'll convince her," Muezza said.

"That man is hopeless," Soraya said.

"I'm telling you, Bygul saddled us with an unmatchable," Muezza said.

"Loosening Reaper's towel should have worked," Soraya said. "I can't understand why it didn't."

"Probably because it required someone with more empathy than Isana Meier," Tivali said.

"Or someone who hasn't been scratched as often as she has," Muezza said.

"True," Soraya said. "I guess when you're used to being scratched on a regular basis, you probably don't have much sympathy for someone who gets scratched just the once."

"Especially when that someone is a man-baby who's wailing and whining," Tivali said.

"It was pretty funny though," Soraya said.

"Personally, I enjoyed watching the bear chase Reaper all around the room," Muezza said. "It's always fun to see earth-bound cats showing humans who the boss really is."

"Yeah, that was hilarious," Soraya said.

"Funny or not, I have no idea how we're going to match

that man with anyone," Tivali said. "He can't even convince a woman who works in cat rescue, who's overrun with cats needing homes, to let him adopt some kittens. The man has more money than most of the gods and she won't even let him have a cranky, old cat. This mission is doomed."

Four

"I'VE COME UP with a plan," Kate announced when Nick walked into their offices the next morning.

"Oh, great. This should be good."

"Isana already knows you, but she hasn't met Ryan, Pete or Lyle. So we'll have one of them go in and try to adopt the dog. Then we'll give it to Maggie for Christmas."

"Dude, maybe you should rethink this whole idea. What if Maggie doesn't want a dog? What if she's allergic? What if the cat decides to fight the dog?"

"Oh, I'm sure Genghis Khat will fight the dog. It'll be all kinds of entertaining, just like when he took Jackson for a ride."

Nick snickered. "That *was* hilarious."

"I think we should send Ryan first."

"If Ryan comes back with a cat, I'll never forgive you."

"Why would he come back with a cat? We're sending him after the dog!"

RYAN WASN'T SURE HOW HE'D BEEN ROPED INTO this situation. All he'd done was show up for work as usual and the next thing he knew, his boss's mate was sending him on a very important mission.

At least he'd managed to convince her to let him finish the car he'd been working on. Otherwise, they would have gotten even more backed up than usual.

As it was, Jefferson had been annoyed with Kate for pulling Ryan from the shop early to go on this ridiculous quest.

She'd given him a highly specific description of a dog and orders not to leave the rescue center without him.

The only good news about this mission was that the cat rescue was located in the middle of Pleasantville, a human town, thus reducing the likelihood that anyone from his pack would see him entering the place.

Dragging in a deep breath for courage, he made his way inside.

Two women stood behind the counter, talking with a woman. There was a young boy at the woman's side who turned and stared at Ryan when he walked in.

Ryan stared back.

Long minutes later, it occurred to him that he was in a stare down match with a kid who couldn't be more than ten years old.

Still, the wolf inside wasn't going to let him look away first. This kid was going down.

Just when Ryan was convinced he might end up spending the entire day there, the kid bared his teeth and made a fierce face.

It would have been more impressive if the kid had fangs.

Sadly, it appeared he was hampered by his humanity.

Ryan lifted his top lip and bared a single fang.

The boy's eye got huge and he jerked back. He slid to the other side of his mother, then peeked out at Ryan again.

Ryan grinned at him.

The boy sent him a tiny smile, then looked away.

A few moments later, the woman walked out of the center her boy trailing behind, throwing glances over his shoulder at Ryan all the way.

"You do realize they were human, right?" At first glance, Ryan had assumed the speaker was older than she was based on her white hair, but now he realized she was probably in her mid-thirties at most.

Interesting.

"I'm here about a dog," Ryan said, ignoring her question about the humans.

Both women looked surprised.

"But we're a *cat* rescue."

"Sarah." The other woman put a hand on her shoulder. "Did Underdog Rescue send you? Just because we agreed to house a few of their dogs doesn't mean we have the time to handle their adoptions for them."

"Isana, I said it was no problem."

"Fine. Fine. But they'd better start sending some cat people our way."

"Come along. I'll show you where the dogs are."

Ryan followed Sarah through a door into another reception area, this one empty. The silence was broken by the faint sound of dogs barking.

"This used to be a veterinary clinic that also offered boarding for dogs before we bought it." Sarah explained as she led him past a number of examination rooms, the sound of barking growing louder with every step. "We have a couple volunteers who come in and use the clinic to administer vaccinations and to spay and neuter our cats, but the kennels at the back of the clinic go unused." She pushed through a swinging door that led to a giant room with kennels lining the walls. "I was kind of glad Underdog Rescue asked us for help. The kennels have doggy doors that lead outside into a run. It's good to see all of this space being used again."

All of the kennels appeared to be empty, though the sound of barking continued.

'The dogs must all be outside." Sarah walked across the room and pushed open a steel door. She used her foot to shove a rock against the door to hold it open. "Come on. You can meet the dogs."

Ryan's attention had already been caught though.

One of the kennels wasn't empty after all.

Inside a large dog was lying, head on his paws, eyes on Ryan. He was pitch black and had the saddest of eyes.

"Well, hello, there, buddy, what's up with you?"

Sarah came back inside. "That's Cujo. I don't know why anyone would name him that because he's the sweetest dog of the lot. He's just sad because his owner died and no one in the family could take him."

MASON DECIDED THERE HAD TO BE SOME BENEFITS to being in charge. He had his assistant cancel his final meetings of the day and escaped the office in favor of the cat rescue center.

He wasn't sure why he couldn't stop thinking about the bear-not-bear, but when he wasn't thinking about the kittens, he was picturing all that white hair and remembering the bear-not-bear's scent.

The mystery of it was driving him mad!

He'd hinted repeatedly throughout his afternoon of volunteering, trying to figure out what animal smelled like a bear, but wasn't, but she'd refused to share. In fact, for the most part, she'd ignored him.

Including when Reaper had tried to scrape off his face.

He couldn't believe how mean she was!

He kind of liked it.

When he arrived at the center and found Isana standing at the reception counter, he was thrilled.

Sarah was nowhere in sight.

Even better.

"Did you miss me?"

She jumped and glared at him. "Like an itchy rash. What are you doing here?"

"I told you I'd be back. I'm here to adopt my kittens. I also brought some Bear Necessities, just in case. This countertop should do nicely." With that, he began unpacking the box he'd brought with him.

Box of donuts.

Platter of cookies.

Homemade breads.

Giant platter of fish lasagna.

Crockpot full of—

"What on earth is all of this?" Isana exclaimed.

Before he could explain, the door to the clinic opened and Ryan, of all people, came through it, leading a dog on a leash.

"What are you doing here?" Mason demanded.

"Are those Bear Necessities?" Ryan made a beeline for the countertop and grabbed a handful of cookies. "You and

Kate are the best people I know." His words were mangled a bit due to his mouthful of crumbs, but Mason still understood him.

"Ryan's adopting Cujo," Sarah told Isana. "Here's his application paperwork and his credit card."

Isana stared at Ryan who was busy scooping lasagna onto a plate, then at Mason who was trying to decide whether he wanted to start off with some bread or with some cookies—maybe he should just go with both—then back to Ryan, who was now gagging and spitting out Mason's delicious fish lasagna—*wolves*. They had no taste whatsoever.

"You two *know* each other?" Isana demanded.

"Well, yeah, he works for my brother-in-law," Mason said.

"As in the mate of your sister, Kate?" Isana demanded. "This is unacceptable. You tell that Kate Worcester that she doesn't get to send her stooges in here to adopt pets on her behalf."

"Hey, I resent that. I'm not a stooge and I happen to be adopting Cujo on my own behalf." Ryan dumped his plate of rejected lasagna into a trash bin and grabbed a new plate that he started piling high with cookies and breads.

Damn wolf.

If Mason had known he'd be there, he would have packed more necessities.

"Right. And I suppose you didn't come here planning to adopt a different dog?"

"No idea what you're talking about."

The wolf was a terrible liar. Mason had a feeling even Isana could tell he was full of shit.

"Fine," Isana said, "but we're not a dog charity. We're a cat rescue. Therefore, if you want to adopt *that* dog, you have to take a cat with him."

"What?" Mason and Ryan roared at the same time.

"I don't need a cat. I don't want a cat," Ryan whined.

"*I* want a cat," Mason snapped. "In fact, I want four. How come you're letting *him* adopt a cat and not me?"

"Sarah, take Cujo back to his kennel."

"No!" Ryan exclaimed. "He wants to come with me."

"Then I guess you'd better go choose a cat," Isana said.

Ryan glared at her.

"Look I've got forty-two cats needing a home. The least you could do is check them out."

"Did you lose one?" Mason exclaimed. "You had forty-three yesterday."

"A mother and her son adopted one a little over an hour ago," Sarah said.

"She'd better not have stolen one of my kittens," Mason said. "Or Reaper. She didn't take Reaper, did she?"

Sarah and Isana stared at him incredulously.

"Only a bear would want that cat," Sarah muttered.

"The kittens and Reaper are still here," Isana said, "along with thirty-eight other cats, so let's get on with it, shall we?"

"Fine," Ryan grumbled. "Introduce us to the cats, but

first—" He grabbed another handful of cookies that he added to the pile on his plate.

Isana rolled her eyes. "What's with all the food anyway?"

"It's Wolf Down Wednesday," Mason and Ryan chorused together.

"I almost starved yesterday," Mason said. "By the time I got home last night, my stomach was busy eating itself. Today I came prepared."

"Whatever."

"Come on, Ryan," Sarah said. "I'll introduce you to some of the cats." She headed for the cat tower and the rest of them followed.

The minute the door closed behind them, Mason made a beeline up the ramp to the left until he reached the section of kennels where he'd found the kittens the day before.

Only today the kennels were empty.

Before he could start roaring his rage, Isana called up to him, "They're in the playroom."

Now why couldn't she have told him that before he came bolting up here?

Since he was already halfway there, he figured he might as well check on Reaper before heading back down.

"Oh, man, you do not look happy," Mason informed Reaper when he finally arrived at his set of kennels.

Apparently Reaper was so territorial, he'd been given five kennels on his level, plus the five above his level and the five below it, which meant he had quite a bit of territory to lounge in. And still he growled the minute he saw Mason.

"Hey, don't blame me. I'm not the one who locked you inside this luxurious kennel-palace. Nor am I the one who insisted you needed medicine. I was just drafted to do the dirty deed."

Reaper let out a yowl of annoyance.

"Fine. You can come with me if you behave." Mason waited, but the cat didn't reply. "Does that non-reply mean you *will* behave or that you're just waiting for me to open this cage door and then you'll be turning into a grimmer version of yourself, which is kind of hard to imagine, but still. You gonna behave?"

No reply.

Hmm. "I guess we'll see." Mason unhooked the cage door and slowly swung it open.

Reaper just glared at him balefully.

"Well, come on. We're going to go play with some kittens. Doesn't that sound like fun?"

Reaper stood and stretched, then sauntered nonchalantly toward the cage door.

Mason reached in and scratched him on the head.

Reaper let out a tiny grumble and nudged his hand for more pets.

Mason took that as permission to move forward with his plan and he carefully lifted Reaper out of his cage.

Mason held the cat up so that they could stare into each other's eyes. He pressed his forehead to Reaper's and let out a soft rumble. Reaper replied with a scratchy meow.

Mason settled the cat against his shoulder, latched the cage door closed again, then turned and stumbled to a halt.

Isana was standing against the opposite wall, watching them. "Well, come on then." She pushed away from the wall and led him down the ramp to the main level where the cat playroom was.

"Did Ryan choose a cat?" Mason asked.

"Not yet. I left them in the playroom. Sarah's been bringing cats in to meet them."

"Wait. They're in the playroom with *my* kittens? You're not going to let Ryan choose one of them, are you?"

"Relax. Ryan was adamant that it had to be a full-grown cat, probably a good idea given the size of Cujo."

"Maybe I should just take Reaper back to his kennel. I don't want Ryan choosing him either."

Isana snickered. "Trust me. That's not going to happen."

Mason saw she was right when they reached the ground floor again.

Ryan was relaxing under the tree at the center of the playroom and wasn't paying attention to any of the cats Sarah kept bringing by.

Instead, he was typing away on his phone, pretty much ignoring all the cats.

By comparison, he was constantly petting Cujo, who was lying on his side, nudging Ryan's hand for more pats and stretching out a paw to pat Ryan's cheek.

"They bonded so fast," Sarah said to Isana. "It's truly beautiful."

"Yeah, great, but I need him to bond with a cat," Isana said.

"I know," Sarah sighed. "Do you have any suggestions?"

Isana looked at Mason, who immediately scowled at her. "Not Reaper."

"Fine. What about Midnight?"

Sarah's eyes widened. "Good idea. I'll be right back." She bolted from the room.

"Who's Midnight?" Mason asked.

"A cat who's been living in a cage for three years. He's sweet as can be, but pitch black, which makes him harder to adopt out."

"Why?"

Isana shrugged. "It's the black cat syndrome. They're just much harder to place."

Mason frowned. "None of my cats are black."

Isana grinned. "That's okay. They need homes too."

At that moment, Reaper let out a low-pitched yowl.

"Sorry, Reaper. Let's go find the kittens, shall we?"

ISANA REALLY DIDN'T WANT TO LIKE THE BEAR, mostly because he was a bear, but also because she was very much afraid he might be her mate.

It was difficult not to like him when he sat and played with kittens though or spent time chatting with a cranky tomcat, trying to convince him to submit to being petted.

At this point, she was pretty convinced Mason would make an excellent cat dad, but that didn't mean she was willing to admit it just yet.

The bear would just get a swelled head if she gave in too soon.

Still, it was hard to resist the man, especially when he kept tugging on her heart strings like he was at that very moment.

Mason was now surrounded by cats and kittens—the three he'd chosen plus a number more. He was playing with all of them, petting them, tossing balls for them to chase, waving cat wands of fabric in front of them, leading them this way and that, almost like a pied piper calling his charges.

The only one not mesmerized was Reaper.

Instead of playing, he was perched at the top of a cat tree, not far from where Mason was playing with the kittens, and was observing the entire room, almost like a guard kitty standing sentry over his charges.

At that moment, Cujo came loping through the area with Midnight on his back.

It was only because Isana had been looking at Reaper at that very moment that she saw what happened next.

Reaper let out a yowl and leapt from the cat tree.

For one single moment, he was airborne, then he slammed into Midnight and the two of them tumbled to the floor.

Reaper landed on top of Midnight and swatted him in the face, then leapt up and onto Cujo's back. There he settled and stared down at Midnight with a superior look on his face, as if to say this was now his dog.

Midnight shook his head, climbed to his feet and yowled.

Ryan hurried over, picked Midnight up and murmured soft words of comfort as he glared at Reaper.

Mason let out a short whistle, Reaper whirled and jumped down to the floor. He sauntered unhurriedly over to Mason's side where he began grooming one of the ginger kittens.

"Wow," Ryan drawled out the word.

Isana chuckled. "Now you know why Sarah said only the bear would want Reaper. So I take it you're going to adopt Midnight?"

Ryan looked surprised, then glanced down at the cat in his arms, then over at Cujo, who hurried to his side and leaned against his leg.

Midnight stretched out a paw and patted the dog on the head.

Ryan grinned. "Yeah, I guess I am."

"Awesome," Sarah exclaimed. "Let's get the paperwork done, shall we?"

They hurried out while Isana tried to avoid Mason's glare.

"You're not going to make him volunteer to earn the right to adopt one of your precious cats?"

Isana shrugged. "We don't need a volunteer anymore. We have you." She turned her back so that Mason wouldn't see her struggle to keep from laughing.

"Oh, that's nice."

"You'd better get started. Those litter boxes won't clean themselves, you know." She hurried toward the door. "I'll be back as soon as I'm done processing Ryan's adoption paperwork."

Isana was driving him crazy.

Mason couldn't decide if he was more annoyed that she still hadn't agreed to him adopting his cats or that she seemed completely unaffected by him, whereas he could barely concentrate on anything else whenever she was around.

He hurried through the tower, scrubbing out kennels, refreshing food and water and scooping litter boxes. While he worked, he munched on Bear Necessities and occasionally shared tiny morsels of fish with the occasional cat.

Isana caught him, though, and that was the end of that.

"Sorry, Larry," he said to a gray, striped cat. "No fish for you."

The best part of the job was spending time with the cats and getting to know each one of them. There were so many and they all had different personalities from fun and energetic to sweet and skittish to hissing and cranky.

No matter what, though, he made sure to talk to each one and to pet as many as he could.

By the time Isana returned to the tower, all the stresses of his day at the office had disappeared under a barrage of kitten meows and purrs. "I think I might be in the wrong profession."

"What makes you say that?"

"I'm in love with your cats. They're so soothing."

Isana grinned. "Yeah, it's a pretty good gig. Doesn't pay anywhere near as well as CEO of a corporation though."

"Eh, money's overrated."

"Uh-huh. So says the filthy rich."

Mason chuckled. "I suppose that's true. And speaking as one of the filthy rich, are you ready to take my adoption fees yet? Or a donation? Or maybe both?"

"You know, I really thought we might be making some progress," Tivali said, "until the idiot bear went and ruined everything."

"What are you talking about?" Soraya exclaimed. "Mason barely spoke with Sarah today. She was too busy helping Ryan."

"What does Sarah have to do with it?" Muezza asked.

"She's his mate. I'm sure of it," Soraya said. "We just have to get them to spend more time together."

"Uh, that's insane," Tivali said. "There's no way Mason's mate is Sarah."

"I don't see why not. Sarah's nice. I think she deserves a mate."

"Isana's nice too," Tivali snarled.

"Yeah, but she hates Mason. Did you hear how she tore into him when he offered her that bribe?"

"What a moron," Tivali said.

"I'm telling you, he's unmatchable," Muezza said.

"Bygul wouldn't do that to us," Soraya said. "I'm sure he would only have us working on a match that's a sure thing and Mason and Sarah are *perfect* for each other."

Muezza let out a scoffing sound. "Mason would be bored out of his mind if we set him up with her."

"Bored!" Soraya exclaimed. "That's so rude. He wouldn't be bored. He'd be *adored*! She's a sweetheart."

"True," Muezza said, "but Mason doesn't need a sweetheart in his life. He'd walk all over a sweet girl like Sarah. He needs someone who will stand up to him and drive him crazy."

"He's right, Soraya," Tivali said.

Soraya sighed. "Damnit. I really wanted to matematch Sarah."

"Oh well. Maybe next time," Muezza said.

KATE COULDN'T BELIEVE IT.

She'd spent all afternoon waiting for Ryan to come back to the garage with the perfect Christmas gift for Maggie and instead he walked into the garage with a cat and some other dog.

"That's not the right dog," Kate exclaimed furiously, glaring at Ryan.

"And *that's* a cat," Nick exclaimed, coming to stand at Kate's side, also glaring at Ryan.

"This is Midnight." Ryan lifted his arms as he said the cat's name. "And this—" he dropped a hand to the top of the dog's ginormous head—"is Cujo."

"You adopted a dog named Cujo?" Pete exclaimed, then burst into laughter.

"Never mind about his name," Kate said furiously. "Who cares about Cujo? He's the *wrong* dog!"

"Well, it's a good thing it's not the right dog," Ryan said, "because if this was the dog you wanted for Maggie, you'd be out of luck. She's mine."

"Well, this sucks," Kate said.

"Yeah, how come they let *you* have a dog?" Nick demanded. "*We* went there first. Now *I* want a dog."

"You can have Midnight," Ryan said.

"I don't want a *cat*."

"*I* want a cat," Mason bellowed as he stormed into the garage.

"Well, you can't have him," Ryan said. "Isana will take back the dog if she finds out I gave you the cat, so just get over it."

"I totally blame you for this, Kate," Nick muttered.

"Get over it? That bear-not-bear *still* won't let me adopt my cats. Plus, she won't tell me what kind of animal she is! She smells like a bear, but isn't a bear and it's driving me crazy!"

"I'll just have to recruit someone else," Kate decided. "Lyle, first thing tomorrow, you're up!"

Five

LYLE HAD NO idea how he'd been roped into this, especially after seeing Ryan return with both a dog *and* a cat.

His mistake had been telling his girlfriend, Heather, all about it when they met for lunch the day before.

He'd told her the story of Kate and the lion-dog she wanted to adopt for Maggie and how she'd recruited Ryan to go to the cat center later that day.

So when Lyle had gotten home the night before, Heather had demanded an update. Had Ryan succeeded in adopting the dog for Kate and Maggie?

Lyle thought the story was hilarious, how Ryan had returned with not only the wrong dog, but with a cat too, so he hadn't hesitated to share this with Heather.

Of course, when he told her that Kate wanted him to try

next, Heather was thrilled. She actually had the next day off, so she immediately began making plans to go with him.

So this was how Lyle ended up walking into a cat rescue in the middle of a human town with his wolf girlfriend at his side.

"Now, remember, Heather, we're only here to adopt the dog Kate wants for Maggie. No other dogs and definitely no cats," he admonished as he opened the door.

"No problem. I can't wait to see this dog. He sounds so cute!"

"Well, isn't this interesting." A woman with white hair approached. "I'm Isana Meier, the director here, and I find it very interesting that so many wolves have been visiting lately. Interested in adopting a cat, are you? Well, come along, follow me." She turned and headed toward a set of doors to the right of the lobby.

"Oh, no, sorry." Lyle hurried after her, Heather at his side. "We're actually interested in—"

Isana whirled and snarled, "Cats first." She flung open the doors and ushered them into a giant tower room.

"Wow." Lyle and Heather stared, mouths agape, at the giant tree in the center of the room.

It was a real tree. Right there, growing through the floor and stretching up toward the dome.

Lyle looked up and realized there were skylights in the dome, letting natural sunlight trickle in.

There were two ramps, one to the left and one to the

right, that appeared to travel around the room, all the way up toward the top of that dome.

"So, tell me the type of personality you'd like in a cat," Isana said.

"Oh, well, um—"

"I want a lap kitty," Heather said, shocking Lyle silent. "Actually, what I really want is a bonded pair. It wouldn't be fair to adopt a kitty and then go off to work, leaving them all alone all day long, so I'd like two kitties. Playful and affectionate."

"I have the perfect cats for you," Isana said. "You're going to love them. Right this way." She led them up a ramp around and around.

As they walked, cats came flying up to the cage doors to get pets as they passed them by.

"They're so cute," Heather said. "I'm so sad I can't adopt them all."

Lyle rolled his eyes. Great. Apparently he'd have to watch his girlfriend for cat hoarding tendencies. Who knew?

The worst part was that they were wolves.

What kind of self-respecting wolf wanted to adopt cats?

"We had barn cats growing up," Heather said. "Every spring, there would be a whole new crop of kittens and I had so much fun playing with them. One spring, I must have been about seven or eight, I sneaked a pair of kittens into my bedroom and I kept them in there for about a month before my parents discovered them. I was quite resourceful. I made litter pans from cardboard boxes that I filled with dirt and I fed them table scraps."

"Did you get to keep them?" Isana asked.

"I did. When my parents saw how attached I was to the kittens, they took them to the vet and got them all their shots. I named them Spooky and Spike. They even went away to college with me. We were inseparable until they passed away at ages fourteen and sixteen."

Lyle hadn't known any of this.

"That's the worst part of pet ownership," Isana said. "They never live as long as we'd like. Well, here we are. This one is Madison and that one there is Max. They're from the same litter and have been here at the center for over a year now."

"Why so long?" Lyle asked.

"They're black cats, honey," Heather said. "Black cats never adopt as fast as other cats, do they?"

"Exactly," Isana said. "Do you want to pet them?"

"Oh, yes, please!"

Lyle didn't even have to see what happened next. It was totally predictable.

Of course, Heather fell in love with the two cats, who were almost indistinguishable from each other. The only differences came in the form of a single white toe on Madison's left front paw and a tiny white dot on Max's nose.

"They're so precious," Heather crooned as she cradled Madison in her arms. "She's so soft."

So was Max, not that Lyle was about to admit it or anything.

Instead, he stoically waited for Heather to finish fawning over the cats, so that he could go find Kate's dog, then fill out the adoption paperwork for three animals instead of one, pay the adoption fees and get on with his life. A life that now included deciding where they would stash the litter boxes and how they would combat the cat fur.

It took a while, but they finally made it to the dog side of the center, where Lyle repeated to himself as they walked through the deserted animal clinic, the details of Kate's description. There was no way he was falling for any other dog. He was there on a mission.

Golden fur, looks like a lion, ginormous paws.

Golden fur, looks like a lion, ginormous paws.

Golden fur—

Ruf! Ruf! Ruf! Ruf! Ruf!

"Oh my gosh, he's so cute," Heather squealed as she fell to her knees.

"What is it?"

Isana chuckled. "Some sort of terrier mix, we're not sure. He won't ever get much bigger than that."

The dog leapt onto Heather's lap, then bounded out of it to race around her and Lyle, then jumped back onto her lap, then raced around again. This time, the dog stopped in front of Lyle, stood on its hind legs and scrabbled at Lyle's pants.

Lyle chuckled and settled down on the floor beside Heather. He scooped the dog up, which was met with ferocious excitement as the dog lunged forward and began licking Lyle's cheeks, nose, forehead, chin and pretty much anything else he could reach.

Lyle laughed and passed him to Heather then watched as she crooned and pet and loved all over that silly dog.

Without too much regret, he got to work adjusting his mental plans once more, this time making room for a dog bed and a dog crate.

MASON LEFT WORK EARLY. HE'D BEEN THINKING about Isana and the cats all day *again*.

The worst part was knowing he'd offended Isana with the offer of a donation, something he just didn't get.

He had money, so why shouldn't he share it with people and causes he cared about?

Still, he had to figure out how to make it up to her. Otherwise, he'd never convince her to let him adopt his cats.

If only he knew what her animal was. If he could figure that out, he'd probably know how to woo her.

For example, if she really was a bear, he'd try honey, but since she was a bear-not-bear, he was at a loss.

He walked into the center and screeched to a halt.

Lyle, the traitor, was standing in the reception area with his girlfriend, Heather. They were each holding a cat carrier and Lyle had the leash of a dog in his other hand.

Seriously?

Mason stormed forward, leaned over and peeked into each of the carriers.

"You're letting *them* adopt Madison and Max?" he demanded.

"Hey, Mason," Heather said. "What are you doing here?"

"I volunteer here," Mason said. "I also have a vested interest in four cats at this center, but *that woman—*" he glared at Isana "—hasn't seen fit to allow me to adopt them yet."

"Oh, we still have to have a home visit once the cats are settled, just to make sure things are going well, but then the cats are ours," Heather assured Mason. "Don't worry, I'm sure you'll get your cats in time. Isana just has to make sure every cat goes to a good home."

"Exactly," Isana said. "Thank you, Heather."

"Well, we're headed out," Lyle said. "Gotta get our new family members settled in."

"Good luck, Mason," Heather called as they walked out the door.

Mason didn't answer. He was too busy glaring at Isana, who was busy shuffling papers and ignoring him.

Well, two could play that game.

He stormed over to where he'd set his boxes of Bear Necessities and started unpacking them.

Cinnamon rolls.

Brownies.

Bear claws.

Popcorn balls.

"Oh, hey, Mason." Sarah came in from the clinic side of the building. "How's it going? Oooh, bear claws. Yum." She grabbed a pastry and took a bite, then froze and stared at Mason. "Wow. Isana, you *have* to try a bear claw. I've never tasted anything so delicious in my life."

"It's a family recipe," Mason said. "One only shared with other *bears*." He sent a pointed look Isana's way. "It's really too bad your boss doesn't admit to being a bear. If she did, I could share the recipe with her, but since she insists she's *not* a bear—"

"*I am not a bear!*"

"—as I was saying, since she continues to insist she's not a bear, well, I'm afraid you guys are out of luck. When they're gone, they're gone."

Sarah let out a huge sigh. "Maybe, Isana, you could—"

"*I am not a bear!*"

"Okay, okay, sheesh. I just came in here to let you know I spoke with Brad over at Underdog Rescue."

"Uh-huh. What'd he want now?"

"So, the thing is they're actually quite thrilled we've managed to adopt out two of their dogs. So now they're wondering if we'd be willing to rent them the kennels on a permanent basis. They'll pay more rent if we agree to continue handling adoptions for them."

Isana scowled. "I'll think about it. We'd need to hire at least one more person though because this is getting a bit much for just the two of us."

"Agreed. Thank goodness we've had Mason the past two days. We'd be swamped otherwise. Thanks again for helping out, Mason."

"No problem. Is that what this is about? You're keeping my cats hostage so I'll keep volunteering?"

Isana rolled her eyes. "Don't be ridiculous. It's because you're a bear. I told you that."

Mason scowled. "That makes no sense! I know you say that you're not a bear, but you smell like a bear which means you're probably a bear. Which also means that you've been taking care of cats for years so obviously bears can be trusted around cats."

"How many times do I have to tell you?" Isana exclaimed. *"I am not a bear!"*

Mason threw up his hands in the air. "Fine. Fine. You're not a bear. Can I *please* adopt my cats now?"

BYGUL HADN'T CHECKED IN WITH TIVALI AND THE others since he'd presented them with their Mason mission. He'd been busy helping cats left homeless after a hurricane reunite with their families or find new ones if necessary.

It was heartbreaking work and he was exhausted.

However, he knew he really needed to check in with his trainees, if only to make sure they weren't destroying already existing matches.

You never knew with those three.

He could arrive and discover they'd managed to break up Jefferson and Kate or even worse, Jackson and Maggie.

It took longer than he expected to track down his trainees. He'd expected them to be at The Worcester Group, but everyone there was talking about how Mason Worcester kept leaving early to go visit some cat rescue in a human town called Pleasantville.

That was an interesting development for a bear known for never leaving his own town.

Bygul was now officially intrigued, especially once he arrived at the cat rescue center and had a frontline view of all the drama happening there.

"Bygul," Tivali exclaimed. "What a surprise."

"Yes, well, I'm just checking in. I don't have a lot of time, but I thought I'd stop by and see how's it going."

"We're failures," Soraya wailed. "Epic failures!"

"What? Surely not."

"We are! I wanted to match Mason with Sarah, but Tivali and Muezza said he'd walk all over her, so then we thought maybe Isana, but there's no way that romance is ever getting off the ground. Isana hates him! We're terrible at this, Bygul."

"Oh, I'm sure it's not that bad." Bygul crossed the room and peeked into a side office where Mason and a woman—this Isana, perhaps—were squared off against each other, arms crossed.

Huh. That was some decidedly hostile body language.

Oh, well.

At least it wasn't any of his former matches going at each other. With these three, you never could tell whether they were going to help a match along or completely annihilate it.

"Don't worry so much," he said to Soraya, even though from what he could tell, there was plenty to worry about. "There are always sticky moments in any romance. You just have to get to the other side. If they're meant for each other, it'll all fall into place. Trust me."

"Are you sure?" Soraya asked.

"Positive."

Muezza made a scoffing sound and Tivali just stared at him suspiciously, but Soraya looked relieved.

Bygul should probably feel guilty since the truth was the situation didn't look good at all, but he really couldn't find it in himself to care, not if it meant he'd never have to train another group of cats to matchmake again.

Even though Mason seemed a really nice guy and probably deserved both a cat companion *and* a love match, Bygul simply didn't have the time to continue training and mentoring incompetent cats.

He'd taught them all he could and now it was up to them. Either the cats would fail and he could get on with his life or they wouldn't fail, in which case, he might be expected to train another group of cats.

Dear goddess, he hoped they failed.

Six

KATE WAS FURIOUS. She couldn't believe Lyle hadn't come to work at all the day before.

He'd even ignored her phone calls and texts.

When she'd asked Jefferson what was going on, he'd just grinned and said, "Lyle's spending the day with his girlfriend," which was *not* the agreement.

Lyle was *supposed* to be adopting Kate's dog and bringing him to her, not hanging out with his girlfriend.

This was why Kate demanded, "Where's my dog?" the minute Lyle walked into the garage the next morning.

Lyle ignored her question and made a beeline for the Bear Necessities table where he started piling pastries onto a plate. He shoved a cake donut in his mouth and set about making himself a cup of coffee.

"Lyle!" Kate exclaimed.

"What?" His voice was muffled due to the donut.

"Where's my dog?"

"What dog?"

Kate gasped. "What dog? The dog I sent you to Pleasantville to adopt. The dog for Maggie!"

"Oh, that dog. I didn't see him there, sorry."

"What do you mean you didn't see him? Did you even look?"

Lyle let out a huge sigh, set down his coffee cup and turned to face Kate.

She took a step back at the look on his face. "What's wrong, Lyle?"

"What's wrong?" He stalked across the office toward her.

At that moment, the office door opened and Pete and Ryan trooped across the office toward the Bear Necessities table, but Kate was too focused on Lyle to respond to their greetings.

Lyle seemed awfully upset, which was pretty unusual for the laidback wolf.

"Do you know what I spent my entire day yesterday doing?" he demanded.

"Um, no."

"I spent hours at a cat rescue center in the middle of a human town, then I spent hours inside a human pet store buying cat food and litter boxes and cat toys and dog beds and dog food. Do you know why I was buying those things, Kate?"

"Because you adopted my dog for Maggie?" She asked hopefully.

"Not even close," he said. "But I did adopt a toy dog. Do you know why they call them toy dogs?"

Kate shook her head.

"Because they're so small they look like little stuffed animal toys. Do you know what else I adopted yesterday?"

Kate shook her head.

"Two black cats."

"Do you know what I didn't adopt yesterday?"

Kate shook her head again.

"The mythical dog that looks like a lion that you sent me there to adopt! You know why I didn't adopt him?" He continued before she could shake her head again, "Because I ended up with two cats and Heather fell in love with the toy dog within two seconds of us entering the dog room. I couldn't risk exploring further in case she found another dog or two or *ten* that she wanted to adopt. So thanks, Kate. Brilliant idea. I now have two cats and a dog while you still have no gift for Maggie." He turned, stalked over to the Bear Necessities table, grabbed his coffee and plate of pastries and stormed out.

The minute the door slammed shut behind him, Ryan and Pete, who had been off to the side, eyes wide, clearly barely containing themselves, finally burst into laughter.

Kate walked over to stand in front of Pete.

His hilarity died instantly. "Oh, no. I've seen the writing on the wall. Everyone who does this little errand for you ends up coming back with a dog and a cat. Lyle just came back with two cats. Well, I am one wolf who has no problem saying no. So here it is: No. No. No. *No.* I will *not* be going to the cat rescue center anytime this century."

AN HOUR LATER, PETE WAS STANDING IN FRONT OF the cat rescue center, wondering how he'd gotten roped into this shit.

He drew in a deep breath for courage and went inside.

He recognized Isana from the description everyone had given him. He'd been hoping to find the other woman they'd described—Sarah—there instead.

Both Lyle and Pete had agreed if it weren't for Isana, they might have managed to escape the cat rescue center with only a dog, but Isana was quite determined and somehow they'd ended up with cats too.

Unfortunately, Pete was doomed to follow in his co-workers footsteps because Sarah was nowhere in sight.

"Another wolf. What a surprise," Isana exclaimed. "Come along. The cats are all in the Cat Tower." She flung open a pair of doors and led the way inside.

It was exactly as Pete and Ryan had described it.

He'd been sure they were exaggerating or just pulling his leg, but there really was a tree in the middle of the tower.

"You go right ahead and wander around. Sarah's in here somewhere. She can answer any questions you have about any of the cats. Just come find me once you've decided which ones you'd like to adopt."

He blanched. Had she just said "ones" as in plural? He didn't want to adopt a single cat, let alone multiples.

What was he supposed to do now?

Rather than head up one of the ramps, he decided to wander the playroom first. Maybe if he hid in there for a while, Isana would forget all about him and he could charm this Sarah woman into letting him adopt just the one dog and no cats.

He walked around the tree at the center of the room and discovered on the other side a wall of windows looking into separate rooms. These must be the individual playrooms Pete was talking about. There were three of them, all in a row, and a cat was sitting at the window of the third room.

He walked down to stand in front of the cat and that was when he saw the woman.

When the others had described Sarah, saying she had reddish blonde hair and green eyes, Pete hadn't thought much about it. Now he realized they hadn't done her justice because he couldn't take his eyes off her.

She didn't realize he was there, so he had the chance to observe her without her knowing. She had a cat toy in her hand, a wand with a long piece of fabric that she was using to entice the cats to play. There were two cats happily chasing her wand, but the third, he still stood at the window, watching Pete watch Sarah.

After long moments of feeling utterly bewitched by her

beauty and the gracefulness of her movements as she waved the wand, sending the fabric swirling this way and that, Pete opened the door and stepped inside.

He drew in a deep breath and immediately knew.

Sarah looked up, eyes wide.

He walked toward her, settled on the floor across from her and told her his name.

And so the hours swept by without either of them noticing.

They played with the cats and talked.

They barely noticed when Isana stopped by to check on them, then left as quietly as she'd come.

Eventually Sarah remembered she had a job to do, so Pete accompanied her all through the cat tower, helping as she fed and gave attention to cat after cat.

She introduced him to all the cats she loved, which was basically all of them, and to the ones she'd completely fallen in love with, which was two. There were more she adored, but two she'd take home with her in an instant if only her apartment complex allowed pets.

When they were finished in the cat tower, they spent time in the reception area, answering the phone and talking about everything and nothing.

They ended the day outside, playing with the dogs, and it was out there, while surrounded by happy, barking, playful dogs, that they had their first kiss.

"OH MY GOODNESS. LOOK AT THAT! I'M A GENIUS," Soraya exclaimed. "We just made our second love match. Or is it our third?"

"But we weren't even *trying* to match Pete *or* Sarah," Tivali exclaimed.

"Speak for yourself," Soraya said. "I've been all about matching Sarah this entire time and I think this is a wonderful development. I'm definitely taking credit for this match."

"Well, if you're taking credit, *we're* taking credit," Muezza said.

"Exactly," Tivali said.

"That's fine," Soraya said. "I have no problem sharing credit. My only question is whether this is our second match or our third."

"Why would it be our third?" Tivali asked.

"Kate and Jefferson, of course! We were definitely there for that match."

"Yeah, but I think technically that match belongs to Bygul," Muezza said.

"Okay, fine, but we do get to take credit for Nick and Ryan, right?"

"Absolutely," Tivali said. "Bygul was completely against that match. We made that happen without him."

"Sweet," Soraya said. "We're on a roll. Two matches down, one to go."

"Yeah, but that one is completely unmatchable," Muezza said.

"He's right," Tivali said. "We'll probably end up having to take credit for *failing* to match the bear."

Soraya scowled. "Well, that sucks. Maybe we should enlist some help from the natives."

"Good idea," Tivali said. "Bygul did say earthbound cats are one of his most valuable tools in making these matches."

"I vote for the kittens," Soraya said.

Muezza let out a growling snort. "Remember Cleocatra? I vote for some of the older, wiser cats."

"How about Reaper?" Tivali asked.

"There's no way that cranky cat is going to help us make a love match," Soraya said.

"Well, the kittens certainly won't be of much help," Tivali said.

"How about we just invite them all?" Muezza suggested.

"All of them?" Tivali and Soraya chorused.

"All of them."

MASON HAD A FULL DAY OF MEETINGS AND couldn't get away early like he had in days past. This made him especially grouchy when he finally arrived at the rescue center and passed Pete and Sarah leaving as he went in.

"Pete didn't have any carriers and no dogs on leashes," Mason said to Isana. "Are you losing your touch?"

Isana grinned. "Not at all. Pete took me aside and asked to adopt Sarah's favorite cats, Shadow and Bandit."

"That doesn't make any sense. Why would Pete adopt Sarah's cats? She's going to be so mad."

Isana chuckled. "Actually, since they're mates, I think she'll be fine with it."

"Seriously?" Mason whirled and raced to the door. He flung it open and stared. Ha, perfect timing!

"What are you doing?" Isana came up beside him.

"Just wanted to see if Pete would manage to convince Sarah to ride his motorcycle."

"Motorcycle? It's barely above freezing outside!"

Mason chuckled. "Like shifters care about a bit of cold."

Isana gasped as the rumble of a motorcycle reached their ears.

A moment later, Pete drove out of the lot, Sarah plastered to his back.

Mason chuckled. "Guess he convinced her. Good for him." He stepped back inside and closed the door behind them. "So what's the plan tonight, sweet Isana?"

Isana blushed. "Same as every night." She turned and headed for her office. "Paperwork, cleaning, cat cuddles."

"How about dinner after?"

She froze, turned and stared at him. "Why?"

"Because I find you intriguing."

"I'm not sure that's a compliment."

Mason grinned. "Trust me. It's a compliment. So what do you say. Dinner?"

"Sure. Why not? But first—chores."

"On it, ma'am."

Isana couldn't believe she'd agreed to go out with the bear.

A *bear*, for heaven's sake!

And especially for dinner. If a date with a bear was anything like family dinners with bears, she'd be at dinner for literally hours.

It could quite possibly take half the night, but even if it didn't, it would certainly last long enough for her entire meal to wear off, leaving her hungry again, all while the bear ate continuously without ever getting full.

She had no idea what she'd been thinking when she accepted his invitation. The bear just sent every rational thought fleeing from her head, especially when he grinned like that. Damn sexy bear.

Isana spent the afternoon putting together a list of excuses for canceling on him.

She planned to use those excuses as they walked around

the tower saying goodnight to all the cats, but things got really strange before she could even pull out one excuse.

It all started with Pepper, a white cat covered in tiny black dots.

She was purring in Isana's arms when Mason got near and Pepper lunged for him.

Isana lurched forward to keep the cat from falling and somehow ended up in Mason's arms.

The first time it happened, she didn't think much of it, but then when two other cats did the same thing and she landed in his arms for the third time, she started to wonder if the cats were all possessed, then she wasn't thinking at all.

Three times was clearly one too many for the bear because the second she collided with him, he swept her into his arms and kissed her.

Heat swept through her and all thoughts were obliterated under the scorching fire of his kiss.

Long moments trickled by as heat spiraled between them.

Dear goddess, the bear could kiss!

It was only the plaintive meow of the cat they'd forgotten that brought her back to herself and gave her the strength to pull away.

And so the evening went, with cats conspiring to send Isana into Mason's arms where he'd kiss her breathless and then they'd go back to work only to repeat that scenario again and again.

By the time they finished their rounds, any excuses

Isana had planned to provide for not going to dinner with Mason were completely lost in the brain fog caused by his kisses.

It was only after Mason had swept her up into his truck and had driven them out of Pleasantville that Isana's thought processes started to come back online.

She was now remembering the myriad of excuses she'd had and was thinking this would probably be a good time to bring one up.

The only problem was she no longer *wanted* to cancel.

Could it be that she was actually falling for the bear?

Could it be that she was beginning to hope he really *was* her mate?

She hadn't decided the answer to these questions before he pulled up into the parking lot of a restaurant.

Oh, dear goddesses in heaven.

She hadn't been paying attention.

Nor had she given proper consideration to the consequences of accepting his invitation.

She should have known that he'd take her back to his home turf, to Worcester Falls.

She should have considered the possibility that he'd take her to the most well-known bear restaurant in the shifter community.

She hadn't considered any of that, though, and now she was well and truly panicked. "Maybe we shouldn't go in, not here anyway."

"What? No. This is absolutely *the* best restaurant in all

of Worcester Falls. They specialize in all types of bear gourmet foods."

"But then, *I'm not a bear*, remember?"

He looked crestfallen. "I keep forgetting. It's because you smell like a bear and if you smell like a bear, you have to *be* a bear. That's just the way it is."

Isana rolled her eyes.

"Truly, though, it doesn't matter. Even if you're not a bear, all the shifters in town agree. The Ice Box is one of the best Shenanigans restaurants around. If you prefer, though, we can drive to a different Shenanigans."

That really wouldn't help because the minute Isana stepped foot into any Shenanigans in the state, every bear she was related to would know she was dating a grizzly.

She really was an idiot for agreeing to this, but fine. She might as well get it over with.

"I'm sure this will be just fine."

"Are you sure?" Mason beamed at her.

"Absolutely."

As it turned out, it wasn't fine at all.

In the beginning, everything was wonderful, full of romance and laughter with Isana falling deeper under Mason Worcester's spell.

It was a truly lovely evening.

Until suddenly it wasn't.

"YOU KNOW WE'RE GETTING PRETTY GOOD AT this," Soraya exclaimed.

"Are you crazy?" Tivali exclaimed. "Those polar bears just threw Mason Worcester through a window!"

"Yeah, but think about all the progress we made up until then!"

"She has a point," Muezza said. "The cats *were* more effective than expected."

"And let's not forget *why* the polar bears tossed him out the window."

ALL THINGS CONSIDERED, EVEN THOUGH IT WASN'T exactly the first date he imagined, Mason felt the night was overall a success.

After all, it wasn't often a woman stood between you and five pissed off polar bears.

It all began innocently enough.

Mason couldn't help but notice that all the wait staff in The Ice Box seemed to recognize Isana the minute they walked in the front door.

He also didn't miss the slight shake of the head Isana sent the hostess when she started to greet them.

From there, everyone acted like they didn't know who Isana was, but that was clearly just them pretending because *everyone* was inordinately interested in the two of them.

As they ate, the wait staff came to their table much more frequently than they visited any other table, to the point that Isana eventually snapped, "We're fine. Don't come by again unless you're delivering more food for the bear."

And this was why Mason had decided Isana Meier was the perfect woman for him.

She understood his appetite and though she rolled her eyes every time he unpacked his boxes of Bear Necessities, she never complained that he'd taken over her countertop for them.

She also didn't give him a hard time when he constantly visited that same countertop to get more necessities nor did she protest when he ate his way through the job from the minute he arrived until they minute he left.

She understood what it meant to be a bear.

Which had him even more convinced that she was a bear herself.

The evidence was piling high.

Exhibit A: she smelled like a bear.

Exhibit B: she understood bears.

Exhibit C: she was clearly well-known at the most famous bear establishment in Worcester Falls.

Little did Mason know, there would soon be an Exhibit D involving a bunch of psychotic polar bears.

The employees at The Ice Box were a mix of polar bears and arctic foxes, something Mason had always found to be very interesting. As a grizzly bear, he wasn't too fond of seals, but he did love how those polars prepped their fish, especially the salmon and the trout.

In fact, Mason loved their food so much, he had two accounts there. One was a personal account and the other was a business account under The Worcester Group. As a result, he was used to being catered to at The Ice Box and honestly, treated like a king.

He definitely wasn't used to the wait staff attempting to spy on his dinner dates nor had he ever been surrounded by polar bears halfway through his meal there.

He looked up, surprised to see five huge polar bears scowling down at him and Isana.

Mason bristled at the possessive look on the polars' faces.

"Isana, it's time for you to go home," one of them said.

Mason narrowed his eyes. Was this polar actually trying to lay claim to Mason's date? She was *his* and no one else's.

"Back off, Bryce," Isana snapped.

It was really too bad that Bryce didn't listen and instead grabbed her and dragged her out of the booth.

It was also too bad that when Mason saw the polar's hand on Isana's arm—*his* Isana—the grizzly woke with a vengeance.

THIS WAS WHY ISANA HAD MOVED AWAY FROM Worcester Falls.

In fact, *this* was why she lived in a human town away from shifters entirely.

Okay, so she'd had the thought that Mason should know what he was getting into by dating her, so she hadn't protested too much when she'd realized where they would be eating.

Now, though, she realized that was a severe miscalculation.

After all, she had never, as in *never*, brought a date to a family-owned establishment.

And this right here was why.

Her brothers.

And her cousins.

Were all *bears*.

In every meaning of the word.

Still, she didn't expect Bryce to manhandle her and she *definitely* didn't expect Mason to go into a rage as a result.

And if she were being entirely truthful, she would never predict that Mason would hold his own against the lot of them.

Sure, he might if he were only up against her two

brothers *or* her three cousins, but put them all together and the grizzly didn't stand a chance.

But then Bryce touched her and Mason lost his ever-loving mind.

One minute, Bryce had his hand wrapped around her arm and was dragging her away from their booth, the next he was flying through the air and landing on a table clear across the restaurant.

Isana had no idea how Mason had done it without knocking her to the ground in the process, but somehow he managed to dislodge that hand, set her aside incredibly gently and throw her brother like he was nothing but a stuffed toy.

The rage in the air was palpable in that split second Bryce was airborne, a rage that came not just from Mason, but also from her idiot family when he roared, *"MINE!"*

Isana was pretty sure that up until that moment, her family had just been messing with her, and by extension, with Mason, but the minute the grizzly tried to lay claim to her, playtime was over and the rest of them attacked en masse.

At first, it looked like Mason might go down under the sheer weight of five polars, but then in an incredible burst of strength, he managed to fling the lot of them off so they went in every which direction, collapsing tables willy-nilly.

Isana was so stunned, mouth agape, she didn't resist even a little when Mason dragged her into his arms and caught her mouth with his.

His tongue stole inside and heat washed through her in a massive wave.

She clutched his shoulders and kissed him back, losing track of where they were, who was watching, basically everything.

Then Mason was the one who was airborne.

And so, Isana's first date with the man who just might be her mate ended in chaos, with five polars and a grizzly roaring their displeasure at each other, arctic foxes taking pictures and videos of the insanity, and Isana pacing in front of her family's restaurant, screaming through the window at her idiot brothers and cousins, threatening them with dismemberment if they even thought to step out onto the sidewalk.

Basically, it was just another day in the life of a family of freaking bears.

Oh, well.

Like she said.

It was better if the grizzly knew *exactly* what he was getting into by dating *her*.

Seven

KATE COULDN'T UNDERSTAND what was wrong with these wolves.

She sent each one on a very simple task—adopt a dog, *one specific dog*—and they kept screwing it up!

Not to mention ignoring her.

According to Jefferson, Pete met his mate the day before.

This was awesome news and she was very happy for him.

However, that was *no excuse* not to call in and report the status of his mission.

How hard was it to send a simple text saying, "I got the dog and by the way, I'm mated now?"

But *no*.

Not a single update from Pete the entire day before and now she was stuck pacing back and forth waiting for him to come in so she could figure out whether she still needed a Christmas dog for Maggie.

If he'd failed in his mission, she had no idea who she'd recruit next.

She was out of mechanics!

"Stop pacing, Kate," Jefferson said. "I'm sure he'll be here soon."

"Yes, but will he come in with my dog?"

At that moment, the garage door swung open and Pete walked in, a sappy grin on his face.

Kate's eyes narrowed. "Where's my dog?"

Pete stumbled to a stop, a confused look on his face. "What dog?"

"The dog you were supposed to adopt yesterday!"

"Oh, yeah, that dog." Pete winced. "Sorry, Kate. I kind of forgot to ask about him."

"You what? You—how could you forget the entire reason you went to the rescue center in the first place?"

"Didn't Jefferson tell you I met my mate?"

"Well, yeah, but what does *that* have to do with my dog?"

"I met her at the rescue center. Not the dog. My mate. Her name's Sarah."

"Hold on a minute. Sarah, the one who sent Mason into the clinic where the lion-dog was?"

"Yep, that Sarah."

"Huh. I kind of liked her. She was quiet, but sneaky."

Pete scowled. "She's not sneaky."

"Please. Anyone who manages to send my brother in the

wrong direction without tipping him off is definitely sneaky. In a good way, of course."

"Whatever."

"Anyway, I'm happy you found your mate, but that didn't help me get my Christmas shopping done, now did it?"

"You know, just a thought," Jefferson said, "but you could get Maggie something else for Christmas."

"Are you crazy? The lion-dog is absolutely perfect for her and it's like a gift for Genghis Khat too, which will earn me brownie points with Maggie."

"What do you need brownie points for, especially ones from Maggie?"

Kate shrugged. "You never know when you're going to need a favor from a friend. Anyway, none of that matters because it isn't helping me *adopt a dog!*"

Jefferson sighed. "If you're absolutely determined to get this dog, you *might* consider asking Jackson. After all, he lives with Maggie now, so maybe you should get his opinion on this particular gift."

This idea actually had possibilities.

As long as Jackson didn't try to steal the dog for his own gift-giving. She'd probably have to go with him, just to be sure.

"Actually, now that I think about it, you might suggest Jackson bring Genghis Khat with him. You know, just in case the cat goes psycho when he meets the lion-dog."

Jackson had no idea how he'd been roped into this shit.

He was pretty sure Jefferson was to blame.

They were panthers, for heaven's sake, so why on earth he was driving out to some human town in the hopes of adopting a dog, he had no idea.

"Now remember," his sister-in-law, Kate yelled, trying to be heard over the sound of Genghis Khat yowling from inside his carrier in the backseat. "This is *my* gift for Maggie. You can't steal him from me."

"No problem," Jackson hollered back, "but if Genghis Khat doesn't like him, you're out of luck."

"Okay, sheesh, fine."

Jackson actually thought getting Maggie another pet for Christmas was a brilliant idea. The problem, of course, was Genghis Khat. Jackson would bet money on the cat attempting to destroy any animal thinking to live in his domain.

Basically, Jackson expected this entire trip to be a giant waste of time.

As soon as they arrived at the center, Kate turned to Genghis Khat and said, "Pipe down, would you? We're here and I need to talk to Jackson for a minute."

Jackson wasn't at all surprised when Genghis Khat fell silent. The cat was seriously smart.

"So, listen," Kate said, "the woman in there will probably try to get you to adopt a cat. If you explain that you already have an incredibly territorial one, she might back down."

"Why are you telling me this?"

"Just so you're prepared, you know, for all the possibilities. Anyway, the dog you're looking for looks like a lion."

"Again, why are you telling me this? You'll be right beside me. I assume you'll recognize the dog."

"Oh, no, I can't actually go inside the center."

He had to be hallucinating. "If you're not going in, then why did you insist on coming with me?"

"Because the last three times I sent a wolf to adopt this dog, they adopted the wrong animals. This time, I'm going to be right here to make sure that you exit that building with the right dog."

"If you come inside with me, you can make sure of that in person."

Kate shook her head. "Trust me. Isana, the woman in charge, will refuse to allow the adoption the second she seems me."

"And why is that exactly?"

"Because I made the mistake of telling her this was a gift for Maggie and apparently the woman is anti-gift."

"That doesn't even make sense."

"I know! What kind of person hates gifts?"

"There has to be more to this story. Wait here." Jackson slammed out of the truck and headed into the center.

KATE SET ABOUT GETTING COMFORTABLE.

She figured it'd be a while since Jackson would have to convince Isana to let him see the dogs, then he'd have to find the right dog and then he'd have to fill out the adoption application and pay the fee and then—

The door she was leaning against flew open and she squealed as she lost her balance and almost fell out of the truck.

"You're an idiot." Jackson said as he steadied her.

"What's that supposed to mean?"

"I just spoke with Isana Meier, the director of the center. I explained that I'm Maggie's mate and that I have Maggie's cat with me and that we'd like to see if there's a dog the cat might get along with as a special Christmas surprise. Do you know what Isana said?"

"Get you begone, you evil gift-giver, you?"

Jackson grinned. "Not even close. She said she thought that was a lovely idea and to bring the cat inside."

"You are *shitting* me."

"Nope."

"Are you sure you were speaking with Isana and not Sarah?"

"White-blonde hair, smells like a bear?"

Kate let out a huff. "Maybe it's her less-evil identical twin."

Jackson grinned. He opened the back door and picked up the carrier Genghis Khat was in.

"This makes no sense. She threw me out, yelling that pets aren't gifts!" Kate climbed out of the truck and stormed toward the building. "I hate this woman with a passion right now." She flung open the door and stormed inside.

Isana was leaning against the reception counter, clearly waiting for them.

"You told me pets weren't gifts!"

"That's true I did, but that was before you sent three other wolves to try and con me out of a dog. It was also before you sent in the mate of the woman you want to gift the dog to."

"Why does all that make a difference?" Kate demanded.

"Sending the wolves showed a certain amount of persistence. It was really quite impressive. However, I still wouldn't have allowed any of them to adopt the dog on behalf of someone else. I *will*, however, allow Jackson to adopt the dog on behalf of his cat *if* things go well between the cat and the dog."

"I don't get it," Kate said. "We can't adopt a dog to give to a person, but we *can* adopt it to give to the cat?"

"You, no. Jackson, as a representative of the household where the dog will live, yes."

Kate let out a low growl. "Are you telling me all I had to do was get Jackson and Genghis Khat to come up here and you would have allowed the adoption from minute one?"

"Pretty much."

Kate was speechless.

Jackson chuckled. "Let's go meet this dog, shall we?"

THE MOMENT JACKSON LET GENGHIS KHAT OUT OF his carrier, the cat went about exploring his environment.

Isana had taken them to an enclosed room that had tile floor, baskets full of cat toys and several cat trees.

Genghis Khat wasn't interested in the cat tree or in the toys.

Instead, he was busy sniffing out every corner of the room, making tracks from one end to the other and back again, nose to the floor, sniffing, sniffing, sniffing.

Jackson chuckled and settled down on the floor in the center of the room and just watched.

Kate was pacing back and forth, impatiently waiting for Isana to return with *her dog*.

Jackson thought it was hilarious that she kept referring

to the dog as hers when she clearly planned to give it to Maggie.

At that moment, Genghis Khat raced up to Jackson and butted his head against Jackson's knee.

Jackson chuckled and scratched the top of the cat's head.

Genghis Khat let out a soft rumbling meow, then took off sniffing across the room again.

At that moment, the door opened and Isana walked in, a giant dog at her side.

"Holy hell," Jackson muttered. No wonder Mason thought the damn thing was a lion. It had so much golden fur around its face, it resembled a mane, and it was *huge*. It might even be bigger than Jackson's panther. If not, it was certainly close.

"The paperwork says they think he might be a Tibetan Mastiff," Isana said, "but they're not sure because he was abandoned and in pretty bad shape when they found him. We've been calling him Leo."

"Awww, poor guy," Kate said.

At that moment, Genghis Khat let out a yowl and charged Leo, who immediately flopped down on his belly.

Genghis Khat leapt over Leo's head and landed on his back.

The dog didn't move.

Genghis Khat rolled back and forth on the dog's back, then slowly slithered down to the floor, where he slunk toward Leo's tail and pounced.

Leo still didn't move.

Genghis Khat rolled over, dragging the dog's tail with him, then rolled back, dragging the tail with him again.

Still no movement from Leo.

Genghis Khat leapt to his feet and ran around the dog three times, pausing at his tail to pounce each time, then racing off again.

"Wow. I haven't seen Genghis Khat this animated in, well, ever," Jackson said.

After pouncing on Leo's tail, playing leap frog over his head and his back and climbing onto Leo's head and gently chewing his ear, Genghis Khat finally curled up on the dog's back and went to sleep.

"Right. We're adopting the dog," Jackson said.

"Yes!" Kate crowed.

Isana rolled her eyes. "I'll get you the paperwork."

Fifteen minutes later, Jackson handed back the completed adoption paperwork and Kate handed over her credit card.

"You do realize Christmas is still two days away," Jackson said. "Where are you going to keep the dog until then?"

Kate grinned. "Mason's house."

Isana's eyes narrowed. "Does Mason know this?"

"He will by tonight."

Isana had just finished emailing the adoption paperwork to Underdog Rescue when Mason walked in. She would never admit it out loud, but she was super relieved to see him.

After the way their date had ended the night before, she wasn't sure she'd ever see the bear again.

She certainly wouldn't blame him after her asshole brothers pitched him through the front window of their restaurant, but even if he'd been okay with that, she hadn't exactly shown her best side, what with all the pacing and screaming like a wild woman.

"I could have sworn I just saw that lion-not-lion in my sister's car as I was pulling into the parking lot and she was pulling out." Mason glared at Isana. "Do you have anything to tell me?"

"Nope, I'll leave that to your sister."

"Uh-huh. So what's on the agenda for today?"

"Same as yesterday."

"Excellent. Though I hope you're referring to the kissing and not the smashing through windows."

Isana could feel blood rushing to her face. "I'm so sorry about that. My brothers are such assholes!"

"Eh, it's fine." Mason laughed. "I really can't complain considering I did the same thing to Jefferson when I first caught him kissing Kate."

"Seriously?"

Mason nodded. "Must be a bear thing."

"Or something," Isana muttered.

"And speaking of bears, I knew you were conning me, claiming not to be a bear. I suppose some might say polars are a breed of their own, but still, at the end of the day, you really *are* a bear."

Isana shook her head. "I'm not a bear."

Mason scowled. "Your polar bear brothers and cousins tossed me quite literally out of their restaurant. I think it's pretty clear. You're a freaking bear."

Isana giggled. "If you say so."

He glared at her. "Come on. Tell me the truth. You're a polar bear, right?"

"You'd better get to work if you want to have time for dinner tonight."

Mason's eyes widened. "You mean I don't have to convince you with kisses this time?"

Isana grinned. "Well, I wouldn't say that."

"I told you we were getting good at this! We might actually match our first unmatchable."

"Doubtful," Tivali said.

"Probable," Soraya insisted. "After all, they've been kissing all night and now he's taking her to his house for dinner."

"Yes, but she still hasn't agreed to let him adopt those

kittens. Until she does that, this relationship is doomed," Muezza said.

"Exactly," Tivali said.

"That gives me a brilliant idea," Soraya said.

]

"THIS IS ACTUALLY PERFECT," MASON TOLD ISANA as he opened his front door. "You wanted to make a home visit anyway, to make sure it's a good environment for the cats. This way, we'll kill two birds with one—" His words ended in a shriek when a giant, golden creature slammed into him.

The force made him stagger back.

He tripped and landed flat on his back under the same lion-not-lion creature he'd seen in Kate's vehicle earlier that day.

At least this time he knew it wasn't a lion.

He tried to shove the dog off him, but the dog was too determined to lick every segment of Mason's face that it could reach.

The sound of laughter reached Mason's ears and Isana came into his field of vision.

"I feel like we've been here before," she said to him.

"Yeah, yeah, yeah." Mason shoved the dog back,

bounded to his feet and held out his hand to Isana. "Let's go inside so I can call my sister and chew her out."

Isana giggled and accepted his hand in hers.

He led them into the house and got her settled in the living room. "Give me five minutes." He pulled out his cell and stabbed his sister's name.

Of course, Kate didn't answer the phone, so he left her a voice mail.

"I don't know exactly what's going on. All I know is there's a giant lion-not-lion in my house and he took me down like I was a bunny rabbit. You'd better not be giving this dog to me, Kate Worcester, or you and I will be having words. I'll be bringing this dog to Maggie's tomorrow for our Christmas Eve celebration and you'd better be passing him off to her because my cats will not be happy to come home and discover a dog has moved in, you hear me? All right. That's all. See you tomorrow. Love you. Bye."

ISANA WAS SO CHARMED IN THAT MOMENT, SHE fell the rest of the way into love with Mason Worcester, a bear shifter who adored his sister so much, he couldn't stay angry with her for the length of even one voice mail message. That final "love you" melted her heart.

Then she noticed the kittens.

All three of them, bouncing past the entryway to the living room like they'd lived there their entire lives.

Except Isana recognized these kittens.

"You stole the kittens?" she shouted, leaping up from the couch.

Mason jerked in surprise and exclaimed, "What are you talking about?"

Isana stormed across the living room into the hallway and there they were, rolling across the floor, wrestling with each other.

"The kittens!" She waved her hands at them. "I can't believe you stole them." She leaned over and scooped up the colorpoint.

"I didn't steal them," Mason exclaimed. "You know I wouldn't do that. Kate must have done it when she took the dog."

"Kate didn't steal the dog. She came by with Jackson and they adopted it for Jackson's mate. They didn't even go near the kittens when they were at the center today so she couldn't have stolen them."

"Yeah, well, I didn't steal them either. They were still there when we left tonight, remember?"

"Oh, like one of the richest men in the world can't afford to hire someone to steal some kittens and sneak them into his house."

Mason looked confused. "Why would I do that? Especially when I knew you would be coming over."

Isana had no idea, but what other explanation was there?

"*THAT* WAS YOUR BRILLIANT IDEA?" TIVALI demanded.

"Well, yeah. I figured if Isana saw the kittens in his home, happy and safe, she'd approve the adoption for him. Never mind. I'll put them back."

"No!" Tivali and Muezza shouted, but it was too late.

A split second later, shouts of horror and surprise filled the air in response to the kittens disappearing.

"Are you crazy, Soraya?" Tivali demanded. "Way to freak out the humans."

"Hey, I didn't know what to do. At least this way, Isana knows Mason wasn't to blame."

"YOU KNOW," MASON MUSED OUT LOUD, "I NEVER really believed Jefferson when he talked about how he'd leave Cleocatra at home in the mornings, only to get to work and discover her waiting for him there."

"Seriously?"

"Yep. I always figured the panther was making shit up,

especially since he kept claiming it had to be god magic, but now I'm not so sure."

"Do you think the kittens are back at the center? Or maybe they never left the center at all. Maybe we just had a shared hallucination."

Mason shrugged. "Well, whether it was a hallucination or it actually happened, we should probably go back to the center to make sure the kittens are safe and sound."

In the end, it wasn't quite the second date Mason had planned.

They ended up getting food from a taco truck on their way back to Pleasantville and then spent the evening at the center, eating tacos, playing with cats and kissing.

It may not have been dinner at his house, but in the end, it was still a perfect second date.

Eight

IT WAS CHRISTMAS Eve and Bygul thought it would be a good idea to check on his trainees again.

This time he found them all inside the kitchen of Jefferson and Kate's house. "What on earth are you three doing here? These aren't your targets. They've already been matched."

"We know," Tivali said. "But our targets are expected to arrive at any moment."

"Yes, and we're expecting a mate announcement at any time as well," Soraya exclaimed.

Bygul let out a surprised meow. "Hold on a minute. I thought you said this romance was doomed, that you were epically failing at the matchmaking."

"We were," Soraya said, "but then we recruited the kittens and things got a lot better. There was kissing and everything."

"Well, that's a great start," Bygul said. "My experience has been that once the kissing begins, the match either dies a natural death or it heats up and goes supernova. So which is it?"

"Supernova," the three chorused.

Huh. This was unexpected.

And not exactly good news.

Since it probably meant he'd be training matchmakers in the art of making love matches until the final day of his final life.

On the other hand, he'd have colleagues with whom he could talk about his love matches and compare notes and strategies.

He supposed it wasn't all bad, especially if he could convince the goddesses that one of these three would be better at the teaching gig.

"Oooh, look!" Soraya squealed. "Mason just arrived."

They're here, Kate texted her brother.

Jackson, Maggie and Genghis Khat had just arrived and Kate knew from experience you could never predict how long Maggie's patience would last. When Maggie was done socializing, she would leave and they wouldn't see her again for days.

Therefore, Kate needed Mason to bring the dog immediately.

She didn't understand why he wasn't already there. He
was supposed to be watching for her text so that he could
show up within minutes of Maggie's arrival.

Where are you?

On your front porch, Impatient One.

Tamping down on the urge to squeal, Kate hurried to
the front door. She stepped out onto the porch and grinned
at Mason.

She pulled the door closed behind her, reached under
the rocking chair to the right of the door and pulled out the
box with the giant bow inside that she'd stashed there earlier.

She hung the bow around Leo's neck and arranged the
card so that it clearly showed Maggie's name. "Ready?"

"I'm right behind you."

Kate accepted the leash Mason handed her, turned and
walked into the house with Mason on her heels.

She stepped into the living room and grinned at Jackson
and Jefferson who were standing on opposite ends of the
fireplace, their eyes on Maggie who was entertaining herself
by playing with Genghis Khat.

Kate was about to say Maggie's name when Genghis
Khat whirled away from her and lunged across the floor,
racing toward Leo.

At the last moment, he launched himself into the air and
landed on the dog's back.

Maggie gasped and leapt to her feet.

Genghis Khat stepped in a circle, then settled on the dog's back, facing Maggie.

For a split second, the room was dead silent, then Maggie let out a squeal of excitement and lunged forward.

She fell to her knees in front of the dog and flung her arms around him. "You're so beautiful." She pulled back and grinned at the cat, "And you look so regal riding him like that, Genghis Khat. I love you both so much!" She grabbed the card that had her name on it and turned it over.

Kate had thought long and hard about what to say on the card.

The first thing she'd written was "Merry Christmas, Maggie, from Kate." However, that hadn't seemed quite enough because it didn't really encapsulate the full measure of human effort that had gone into this gift.

So then, in smaller letters, she had added, "with completely incompetent help from Lyle, Ryan and Pete (but it's the thought that counts) and somewhat competent help from Mason and Jefferson, but mostly with truly exceptional help from Jackson and Genghis Khat."

Then, because Kate definitely wanted credit for the gift, she'd added one final thought, "But mostly, as in entirely, this gift is from Kate. Merry Christmas!"

Maggie sniffled a little, then stood and threw her arms around Kate, shocking everyone with the affectionate gesture. "Thank you so much, Kate. I love him." She pulled away and settled back on the floor to stare into Leo's eyes. "What's his name?"

"They were calling him Leo."

Maggie made a face. "I don't see it."

"Uh, he looks just like a lion," Mason muttered.

Kate shoved an elbow into his side and said, "That's what I thought. I figured you could come up with a better name than that."

"Let's see," Maggie said. "He's definitely a boy?"

"That's what all the paperwork said."

"So I guess Queen Elizabark is out of the question."

Genghis Khat growled softly and the dog let out a huffing sound.

Maggie giggled. "*King* Elizabark?"

Genghis Khat growled even louder.

"Okay, okay, that was just a joke. Let's see. It has to be a name worthy of such a majestic looking animal. How about... Spawtacus?"

Kate chuckled. "I like it."

"Genghis Khat and Spawtacus, a match made in heaven," Maggie exclaimed.

Kate grinned.

Success!

Of course, there was one problem with finding the perfect gift and that was realizing she'd never be able to top it.

Oh well.

Totally worth it.

They were all gathered in the living room, talking and laughing, when Kate's phone buzzed again.

As soon as Mason's attention was fully on Cleocatra, who was stalking Spawtacus, acting like she was going to pounce, Kate slipped out onto the front porch again.

This time, Isana was waiting.

Kate ushered her inside, opened the carrier Isana held and scooped the three kittens into her arms. She grinned at Isana and whispered, "Right, let's go."

She led the way back into the living room and headed toward her brother, who was sitting on the floor playing with Cleocatra. "Merry Christmas, Mason." She leaned over and set the three kittens in his lap.

Mason looked overjoyed for a split second, then that joy melted into horror. "You didn't steal them, did you? Isana will never forgive me if you stole them!"

Kate giggled and Isana said dryly, "Don't be ridiculous. Our security is exceptional."

Mason snickered, lifted each kitten for a kiss on the nose, then set them each, one by one, on the floor where Cleocatra hunkered down and glared at them.

Mason stood and pulled Isana into his arms for a kiss. "Thank you, sweet love."

"Hey!" Kate exclaimed. "She's not the one who gave you those kittens. Maybe I'll just take them back and Reaper too."

"Reaper?" Mason pulled away to ask.

"Kate's already filled out all the adoption paperwork and paid the fees on all four cats," Isana said. "You can pick up Reaper after the holiday."

"Aw, you've made my year, sweet Isana mine." Mason kissed her again.

"Hey!" Kate exclaimed. "I say again, Isana's not the one giving you the cats. *I am!*"

Mason laughed, flung an arm around Kate's shoulders and dragged her close, shoving her face into his armpit as he hugged her tight. "Thank you, sister mine."

"Argh! *Mason!*"

BYGUL WAS POSITIVELY STUNNED. HE'D WRITTEN Mason Worcester off as an unmatchable. And now his three trainees had somehow proven him wrong. They'd accomplished a match even he had deemed impossible.

"I have to say, I'm really impressed," he told them. "One of the things about being a good matchmaker is never giving up on your targets. Sometimes it seems impossible. Sometimes you just can't find that perfect match and you have to move on. That doesn't mean you might not find their match years later, when you least expect it though. This match may not have taken years, but it was definitely a difficult one and you three never gave up."

As Bygul spoke, he paced in front of them and watched as his words washed over them and their postures straightened, their ears pricked up and their chins lifted in pride.

"I have a status meeting with the goddesses tomorrow and I'm going to recommend that you three be given full matchmaker status for love matches."

He waited as the three of them lost their composures for a moment and indulged in a bit of cheering. And some wrestling. And a whole lot of grooming.

When they finally came back together, he looked them over with pride.

Perhaps he'd be stuck training new cats for the rest of each of his remaining lives, but for now, he would bask in the glory of having trained three more cats to spread love matches far and wide.

"Congratulations, you three."

"I can't believe I'm finally meeting your kittens," Maggie exclaimed.

Mason grinned. She'd been nagging him ever since he texted her those pictures.

"I've been wanting to meet them ever since I named them."

"Wait, what?" Isana asked.

"Mason texted me for their names when he first met them."

"Why would you have their names?"

"Maggie's really good at naming pets," Jackson said.

"It's true," Maggie said. "I have a gift."

"So the names you made me put on their cages weren't names that *you* created for them?" Isana demanded.

"Of course they weren't," Mason said. He couldn't understand why she would think otherwise. "What do I know about naming kittens? I asked Maggie because she's the expert."

"Now I'm completely curious," Kate said. "What are their names?"

Isana picked up the fluffy orange kitten and showed him to the room. "This is Furcules."

"And this is Purrseidon." Maggie picked up the second orange kitten and showed him off. "This white mark here looks just like a trident."

Isana leaned over to look, then exclaimed, "It does! I never even noticed that."

"And this is Catphrodite." Mason showed off the white kitten.

"Because look at her!" Maggie exclaimed. "She's totally a goddess of beauty who knows how to accessorize."

"Accessorize?" Jackson asked.

"The face, the paws, the tail, the ears! The brown is just perfection against all that white."

"Well, all I have to say is those names are awesome," Kate said with a laugh. "Too bad you can't get a job naming cats, Maggie. You'd make a fortune if you—"

A loud thudding knock came at the front door, making everyone jump.

Isana would know that knock anywhere.

Kate sent her a sympathetic grimace. Obviously she knew the pain Isana lived with on a daily basis.

The only difference between the two of them was that Kate only had *one* brother bear to deal with whereas Isana was lucky enough to have five. The fact that three were cousins and not brothers didn't really signify.

They were still, *all of them*, brother bears.

Brother bears who didn't hesitate to invade as soon as Jefferson made the mistake of opening his front door.

The five of them sort of pushed their way inside and Jefferson just backed up all the way into the living room.

"Well, this is an interesting gathering," Steven said.

"What are you guys doing here?" Isana demanded.

"You abandoned us for Christmas Eve in Greensboro. Of *course,* we had to come see what was up. But don't worry, it's not just us." He grinned. "The rest of the family's setting up outside."

That was when Isana knew her family was going to give the bear a chance to prove himself worthy of her.

She knew this because the arctic fox side of the family had just arrived.

"I'M SO CONFUSED," MASON CONFIDED TO ISANA, his statement a bit garbled from the platter of fish kebabs he was working his way through.

The two of them were standing outside in the snow, watching as Isana's family of polar bears, plus a whole bunch of arctic foxes, mingled with panthers and grizzlies and the many other residents of Greensboro who kept stopping by.

At first, it had just been a few shifters who happened to be in the area and smelled the food.

Then it was a veritable stream of people as word spread that the cooks from The Ice Box were at Jefferson's place cooking enough food to feed an army of bears.

It seemed to Mason as if every employee of the restaurant, both polar bears *and* arctic foxes, were standing in Jefferson and Kate's front yard.

They all moved like a well-oiled machine. Some were cooking, others were serving and the rest were chatting and laughing with the people consuming their food. Then everyone would shift and those who'd been mingling would be serving or cooking and those who'd been working would now be mingling.

"Confused about what?" Isana asked.

"Yesterday your family wanted to kill me. Today they're at my sister's house, cooking for the entire community. This does not compute."

Isana chuckled. "They're bears. What do you expect?"

"Yes, let's talk about your family of bears again and why you seem to *still* think you're not one of them."

"Oh, I'm definitely one of them. I'm just not a bear."

Mason let out a growl of pure frustration.

Isana giggled. "Come on. I think it's time you met my parents."

"Wait. What? Your parents are here? *Now?*"

"Yes and yes. Come on." She caught his hand in hers and dragged him to the biggest grill in the front yard where an absolutely massive polar bear shifter was flipping giant slabs of meat. At his side was a tiny woman who looked so much like Isana, Mason immediately knew she was Isana's mother.

"Mom, Dad, this is Mason Worcester," Isana said. "Mason, this is my mother, Lisa Meier, and my father, Zachariah Meier."

"Pleased to meet you both," Mason lied, trying to sound as if he meant it when in reality, he was quite horrified.

Not that he didn't want to be accepted by Isana's family, just that he was quite terrified it would never happen and would have put off this meeting, as a result, for as long as he could.

Zachariah let out an aggressive-sounding grunt, but Lisa

beamed and stepped around her mate to hold out her hands to Mason.

He stepped forward and she clasped his hands in hers. "I'm so happy to meet you, Mason." She stretched upward as if she were going to kiss his cheek, but that never happened because her mate grabbed her around the waist and set her on his opposite side again.

"Zachariah!" she exclaimed.

He just glared at Mason and grunted, "Mine."

Since Mason completely understood the sentiment and thoroughly respected it, he nodded his head in agreement. "Yours."

The truly impressive part of that encounter was that Mason managed to restrain his grizzly who wanted nothing more than to do the same and lay claim to his own mate by roaring, "Mine!" in his mate's father's face.

It was only as they walked away from her parents, hand-in-hand, that Mason came to his senses and realized what he'd just learned.

He stumbled to a stop and pulled Isana around so she was facing him.

He then leaned forward, placed his nose in the hollow of her neck and inhaled deeply.

Bear was still the overriding scent, polar bear to be exact, but underneath that scent, almost completely buried was the tiniest strain of—

"Arctic fox," he breathed.

Isana giggled. "Exactly so."

He pulled back and stared into her eyes. "Your dad's a polar and your mom's a fox."

"Yep." She glanced around the yard. "I'm related to pretty much all the foxes and polar bears here plus everyone who works at The Ice Box is a relative of one kind or another."

"Wow."

"Yeah. I'm an anomaly. Most of my family, what you smell is what you get, but not me. I'm an arctic fox who smells distinctly like a bear."

Mason grinned. "I find that incredibly sexy. Just one question."

"Yes?"

"Is your arctic fox the size of a fox or the size of a bear?"

Isana rolled her eyes. "Don't be an idiot."

Nine

BYGUL WAS ACTUALLY a bit nervous, which was somewhat shocking, but then he *was* about to meet with the goddesses to explain that most of his trainees had abandoned ship.

The most annoying thing about this meeting was that Freyja wasn't there yet.

Ceridwen and Bastet were, though, and they were demanding answers.

"So?" Bastet exclaimed impatiently. "Did my cats make it or not?"

"And what about mine?" Ceridwen demanded.

"Aw, well, the thing is, Bastet and Ceridwen, most of the cats just weren't interested in making love matches. They had other things consuming their attention."

"So they just stopped attending?" Ceridwen demanded.

"Pretty much."

"So how many completed your course then?" Bastet asked.

"Three."

Silence.

"I'm sorry," Ceridwen said. "Did you say three?"

"Exactly so. Three."

"Out of fifty?" Bastet exclaimed. "That seems awfully low, doesn't it?"

"Well, which three? And were any of them mine?" Ceridwen asked.

"Or mine?" Bastet asked.

"I'm terribly sorry, but none of your cats, Bastet, and none of your cats, Ceridwen, made it to the end."

"Not even one of them?" Bastet demanded.

"I'm afraid not."

"Were they all Freyja's cats?" Ceridwen asked.

"Uh, no."

"No? Well, who are we talking about then?" Bastet asked.

"Are you sure Fannar didn't make it?" Ceridwen asked.

"I'm afraid he abandoned class pretty early on."

"What about Firwen?"

"He made it to our first trip to the earth realm, but then he seemed to lose interest. Honestly, I don't think he cared much for the task of making love matches."

Ceridwen rolled her eyes. "Fair. He's not much for romance, but surely Gwyneira was interested?"

"She was, at least until the first snowfall. After that, we

never saw her again. I assume because she was playing in the snow."

Ceridwen let out a huge sigh. "Well, this is thoroughly disappointing."

"We could spend all day asking names," Bastet said, "when it would be much simpler if you would just tell us who made it, rather than us having to guess."

"Right. They're waiting outside," Bygul said. "If you're willing, I could just invite them in."

"Fine, fine." Ceridwen waved her hand.

Five minutes later, Soraya, Tivali and Muezza stood in front of the two goddesses.

"Are you being serious right now?" Bastet demanded.

"Quite serious," Bygul said.

"Not one of these cats are the cats of a goddess," Ceridwen complained. "Sure, Muezza happens to be companion to a prophet, but that prophet's a *man.*"

"And what is up with the cats of the queens of Egypt?" Bastet exclaimed. "Why are Nefertiti and Cleopatra so special? They're just queens, not goddesses, no matter how much Cleopatra likes to pretend otherwise."

At that moment, Freyja walked in. "So sorry I'm late. I hear we have three graduates from your class, Bygul. How wonderful." She turned to the cats waiting at his side. "Soraya, Tivali, Muezza, congratulations. I know that Nefertiti must be so proud of you, Soraya, and Cleopatra of you, Tivali." She turned to Muezza. "Muhammad will undoubtedly not believe me when I tell him you completed the course. He will be most impressed, I'm sure."

"Yes, yes, but Muhammad has no need to be making love matches," Ceridwen said. "I wonder if he'd be willing to let me borrow Muezza so he can make some on *my* behalf from time to time."

Muezza didn't appear to have any sort of reaction to that suggestion. A pretty laidback cat was Muezza overall.

"I'd ask Nefertiti to borrow you, Soraya," Bastet said, "but you and I both know she'll want something in return."

Soraya let out a tiny rumble of agreement.

"I guess Soraya and Tivali can just go on making love matches on behalf of the Queens of Egypt, though honestly, Cleopatra probably won't even notice," Freyja said.

Too busy traveling incognito and interacting with the masses, Bygul assumed.

"Forget that," Bastet exclaimed. "If they're going to be making love matches on behalf of Egypt, they'll be doing so in *my* name. I'll negotiate with Queen Nefertiti for Soraya's time, but Queen Cleopatra can just suck it up."

Overall, Bygul thought the meeting went quite nicely. He was particularly impressed with how Freyja managed to manipulate Bastet into accepting both Soraya and Tivali as her representatives.

Bastet probably believed that was all *her* idea.

The biggest relief of all though was that Freyja didn't ask for any of the three to work on her behalf, leaving Bygul's position as her top matchmaker and *only* maker of love matches completely intact.

Even better news than that, though, was that none of the goddesses suggested he train any more cats.

Hallelujah to that.

THE FOLLOWING MONTH WAS THE BEST OF Mason's life.

Before he met Isana, he was well-known for arriving at the office just as it was getting light outside and not leaving until darkness had blanketed the land.

Work had always been his life.

Now his life was Isana.

He learned to delegate more just so that he could spend time with her. He continued volunteering at the center and spent his evenings courting his mate.

They went to dinner at The Ice Box once or twice a week just to keep her brothers and cousins from interfering too badly in their relationship, and the rest of the week, they indulged in picnics in the snow and dinners at his place.

The first time she stayed the night, he felt as if he'd won the lottery. He truly was the luckiest man alive.

Isana couldn't understand how she'd gotten so lucky.

Mason was absolutely extraordinary. Even after the holidays, he continued volunteering at the center, despite no longer needing to convince her to let him adopt Reaper and the kittens.

He still showed up every afternoon with boxes full of The Bear Necessities, but now they regularly included some of her favorite foods and fresh flowers, plus quite often, he brought a blanket and candles for picnics in the cat tower.

It was no wonder that one Saturday afternoon after an entire week filled with picnics and cats and kisses from Mason that she decided to close the center early and follow him home.

The anticipation as she drove behind his truck built until she felt as if she was on fire by the time she pulled into the long driveway leading up to his house.

The moment Mason stepped down from his truck and turned to look at her, lust burning in his eyes, she knew this first time was going to be fast.

Thank goodness.

They burst in the front door and fell upon each other, kissing and struggling with their clothes, trying to get rid of them without losing contact with each other.

Finally, they were skin to skin.

Mason lifted Isana and pulled her legs around his hips, nudging her into position. He stepped forward, braced her against the wall and slammed deep.

She arched her back and cried out in ecstasy.

Right there, in the entryway of his home, he took her fast and hard.

She writhed against the wall, clutching his shoulders and whimpering as he worked his way in and out, dragging forward and back, hitting the right spot again and again and again until the world exploded into shards of searing heat and light.

Long moments later, they stood there, her hands clutching his hair, his hands clamped on her ass, both of them breathing heavily, gasping for air.

"Sweet mate," he rumbled in her ear.

"Yes," she breathed.

"Again."

Her heart, which had finally started to settle into a regular rhythm, missed a beat and heat rushed through her.

Her pussy, already soaked, softened further and he sank even deeper with a growling rumble.

The second time was as fast as the first and it wasn't until the third time that they made it out of the entryway.

It was then they discovered that though she was stark naked, he still had on his boots and his jeans were around his ankles.

They had to take a brief pause so that he could extract

himself enough to be able to walk, but the minute he was free, he hitched her up in his arms, hooked her legs around his hips and sank deep again.

The third time happened along the way between the entryway and the top of the stairs.

Every step up had her whimpering in pleasure and by the time they reached the top, they were desperate.

He laid her down right there at the top of the stairs and proceeded to obliterate the world once again.

They did finally make it to his bed, but it was the wee hours of the morning by then and they ended up only sleeping once they got there.

When they woke a couple hours later, though, that was another story.

And so it was just one month after their first meeting that Isana ended up mated to a bear, something she'd always sworn never to do.

And it wasn't just any bear, but a grizzly and a Worcester at that, and it wasn't just any Worcester, but the alpha Worcester himself.

She was pretty amazed at how things had turned out, especially since it was probably inevitable that she would eventually move in with Mason, which meant she would be back in Worcester Falls, living among bears again.

Not to mention the fact that he was now responsible for her falling off the wagon of cat adoption. Sure, technically, Mason was the one who adopted Reaper and the kittens, but when her last cat had died three years before,

Isana had promised herself not to start down that slippery slope again.

Because in her world, one cat always led to two, which often led to three, which could, for those who loved cats as much as Isana did, lead to a houseful of them.

And so she'd kept rigid control of her cat adopting ways and had succeeded in convincing herself that the cats she served at the shelter were cats enough for her.

The key was discipline.

Or at least it was until she met a bear, who quite possibly loved cats more than her, and she mated him.

Now she was on that slippery slope again, this time with him, and it didn't begin with just one cat. It began with four.

Fate truly was a bitch sometimes.

All in all, though, she really couldn't complain.

After all, she'd ended up with a bear who happily volunteered at the center, even going so far as to clean an untold number of litter boxes for her. What said true love more than that?

And he didn't just show true love for *her*.

He also showed it for all the cats, bringing them new cat toys and climbing trees and eventually, adding cat treats to his Bear Necessities boxes, thus earning him the undying love of all the cats at the center.

Even the grumpy ones.

In the end, Isana decided that perhaps fate wasn't so much a bitch as a very clever fox.

And speaking of foxes, there was still one final hurdle they had to overcome and that was for Mason to meet hers.

THE BEDROOM WAS INCREDIBLY COLD WHEN Mason woke one morning a couple weeks after Isana had started spending the night.

A quick glance outside told him they'd received an epic snowfall overnight.

There was white blanketing the land as far as he could see. His truck was buried to the top of its tires and there were snow drifts even taller than it.

He was disappointed to realize Isana had already left the bed, possibly to go in search of coffee.

He waited to see if she'd return, hoping to convince her to climb back into bed, but she never appeared, so he got up, pulled on a pair of jeans and went in search of her.

His house wasn't exactly small so there were any number of rooms where she could be hiding. However, her scent had dissipated just enough to make him think she was no longer inside.

He grabbed a cup of coffee from the kitchen, then wandered out onto the front porch.

He loved this type of weather.

Unlike full-blooded grizzlies, who preferred to hibernate

in the winter, Mason and his grizzly loved to play in the snow.

Unfortunately, he wasn't seeing Isana anywhere.

He was pretty sure she was out there, though, and he was willing to bet she was in her arctic fox form.

He set his coffee cup on the railing, peeled off his jeans and lunged down the stairs, landing in the snow in his grizzly form.

He shook his head and took off running, following the scent of his mate.

Something huge and white lunged up from the snow in front of him and he let out a startled roar.

He toppled backward and stared at the vision hovering above him.

His mate was *not* the size of an arctic fox.

Isana was so excited when her mate came out onto the front porch.

She was crouched low in the snow, just waiting for him to come find her.

She inched forward, belly crawling from the woods where she'd been shaking snow from the trees, toward the porch where her mate stood.

She froze when he suddenly stripped nude and lunged

down the front steps.

He landed in his grizzly form and raced straight for her.

Did he see her?

Her backside wiggled in anticipation.

Almost.

Almost.

Almost.

Now!

She exploded upward, snow flying everywhere, and let out a yip of excitement. *I'm here, I'm here, I'm here.* She leapt all around her mate, who looked a little stunned from where he'd fallen into a snow drift.

I'm here! She leapt on top of him and they rolled around in the snow, wrestling and breaking apart only to lunge back together and wrestle some more.

Finally, she broke free and ran across the lawn and around the house, her mate thundering after her.

It was a truly perfect morning and the start of a beautiful life together.

REAPER WANDERED THROUGH THE HOUSE, checking all the entrances, peering through every window and growling a warning into the night.

All intruders beware! This house belongs to The Reaper,

Guard Kitty Extraordinaire.

Once Reaper was certain his territory was secure, he stalked into the room where his humans slept.

First, he checked on the kittens.

All three were sound asleep in their cat bed.

Furcules and Purrseidon were wrapped around each other while Catphrodite was stretched out on top of them both.

He sniffed each of them, gave them each a nuzzle and a swipe of the tongue, then sauntered over to the bed where the humans were sleeping.

He leapt up and circled them both, searching for the perfect spot.

Eventually, he wiggled his way in front of the female, stretching out against her belly so the man's arm that had been around her waist was now around Reaper too.

Lying there, Reaper listened to the sounds of kitten purrs from across the room and the soft breathing of his human companions, and fell asleep to the realization that his own lost purr had been found again.

Read on for an excerpt from *A Catmas to Remember.*

Excerpt

Bygul wasn't happy about his latest assignment.

He might be the best matchmaker on the Pawsitively Purrfect team, but this case required a miracle worker.

"This particular cat is quite the troublemaker," Freyja informed him.

"He's been returned *seventeen* times," Bastet said.

"And by humans who adore cats, no less," Ceridwen agreed.

"Seventeen—how is that even possible?" Bygul demanded. He couldn't imagine that the director of the center, Isana Meier, had screwed up that many matches. After all, the woman was outrageously protective of her rescues.

"The cat's an asshole," Freyja said.

"Entirely," Ceridwen and Bastet agreed.

"But that's simply the nature of cats," Bygul protested.

Freyja raised an eyebrow. "Yes, but this cat takes it to unprecedented levels."

"He's smart," Bastet said.

"And devious," Ceridwen said.

"And he knows exactly how to make life miserable for his humans," Freyja said. "He's in a league of his own."

Now Bygul was intrigued.

Not that he would admit it, of course. "He can't possibly be that bad. Any true cat lover would put up with all manner of assholery from a cat."

"Not this one," the goddesses chorused.

Interesting.

Bygul did enjoy a challenge, but there were limits. "And how exactly am I supposed to get this cat away from the rescue?" Normally he just took the cats, but those were cats living on the streets, fending for themselves, with no humans to worry about them when they disappeared.

"You're just going to have to work with the humans to find the perfect placement for this cat," Freyja said.

"Have you *met* Isana Meier? Talk about uptight! *She's* the asshole in this scenario. She'll never let that cat be adopted by just anyone."

"Of course not," Ceridwen said.

"And why should she?" Bastet asked. "Every cat deserves the purrfect human."

"Exactly," Freyja said. "So your job is to find that human and somehow get them into the rescue to meet the cat."

"It's not enough that they meet the cat. Isana Meier has to approve their application and believe you, me, that's never an easy—"

"Bears!" Soraya exclaimed.

Bygul jumped a little. He'd completely forgotten the recent graduates he'd trained were in the room.

Great.

Now they'd want to assist in this match.

"Oooh, yes, bears," Tivali said.

"What are you two going on about?" Bygul glared at them.

"Who better to adopt an asshole cat than shifters who are assholes all the time?" Tivali asked.

"I vote for the polars," Soraya said.

"That's a crazy idea," Muezza said.

Bygul completely agreed.

"It's not crazy!" Soraya exclaimed. "It's purrfect!"

"Those polars are always fighting," Bygul said. "Besides, don't you remember how adamant Isana Meier was about bears *not* being an appropriate cat companion?"

"Yes, but that was before she mated one," Tivali said.

"Besides the polars are family," Soraya said. "She'd never deny family."

These cats were delusional.

Isana Meier would deny the goddesses themselves if she deemed them unworthy.

"Well, we'll leave the four of you to figure out the details," Freyja said. "Bygul, you're in charge. If you can't find a match for this cat, I fear for his future."

Great. Way to pile on the pressure. "What's the cat's name anyway?"

"Shredder," the goddesses chorused.

Wonderful.

"No," Mason said.

"He needs a home."

"That may be so, but his home's not going to be anywhere near *my* precious babies."

Isana rolled her eyes. "They're not even kittens anymore. They're fully grown and thus, are capable of defending themselves."

"Against Shredder the Destroyer?" Mason demanded.

"Stop calling him that!"

"Look, you know I love cats, but *that* is not a cat."

"Really, Mason?" Isana glared at her mate. Some days, she doubted her own sanity. She'd had one rule and one rule only her entire life: *no dating bears.*

And now look at her!

Mated to one.

For life.

A stubborn, clumsy, rampaging, irrational *bear*.

"If he's not a cat, then pray tell, what is he?" she demanded.

"Best guess? A demon from hell."

Isana groaned. "Can't we just discuss this? I've exhausted every cat lover I know in three counties. *Everyone's* heard about Shredder. No one's willing to take him in."

Mason just stared at her.

"What? What's that look supposed to mean?"

He didn't answer.

"What?"

He just kept staring.

She *hated* it when he did that. "Just say it already!"

"I've already said it a thousand times."

"Oh, no. Forget it. I already told you, no. We're not foisting Shredder off on the shifters."

"I don't see why not. You've adopted out to shifters before."

"Those were exceptions, not the rules. You know I prefer adopting out to humans, Mason."

"Which makes absolutely no sense whatsoever."

"It makes perfect sense."

"Not to anyone who isn't you."

Isana let out a tiny growl of frustration. "Fine. Who would you suggest then?"

Mason grinned. This was going to be fun.

Bryce had worked a double at the restaurant the day before and was sound asleep when the pounding on his front door began.

He let out a roar of rage that rattled the windows and shook the floor, but didn't bother to get out of bed.

His roar was usually enough to send even the most determined packing.

Unless they were family.

Or insane.

Or both.

The pounding began again, which told him it was probably family.

Either that or the nutcase next door.

Either way, he was ignoring them both.

He pulled a pillow over his head and tried to ignore the relentless pounding.

It finally stopped.

He smirked a little as he sank back into sleep.

Bam! Bam! Bam! Bam bam bam!

Bryce jumped so hard, he almost fell out of bed, then leapt to his feet with a roar.

Family!

It had to be family.

The woman next door might be crazy enough to risk his wrath, but he doubted she had the strength to make the windows rattle the way they did with that last knock.

It was probably Isana.

Only his sister would have the audacity to continue knocking despite it becoming clear he had no intention of answering the door.

"Bryce, we know you're in there!"

Yep. That was his sister all right.

There was a reason he'd taken away her damn key.

Apparently, that wasn't enough though.

He should have moved.

Out of the country.

Bryce stamped across the room and flung open the window. "What the hell is wrong with you?" He couldn't see his sister because the roof of the porch obstructed his view, but he knew she was there.

The roof shook a little as Isana stamped down the stairs, turned and glared up at him. "Get your ass down here, Bryce Meier. Right now."

"I worked a double yesterday. Now go away." He pulled his head back inside the house, slammed the window and turned away, fully intending to climb back into bed and continue ignoring his sister.

Bam! Bam! Bam! Bam! Bam! Bam!

Hands on hips, Bryce glared at his bed.

Surely she'd give up.

Any minute now.

Bam! Bam! Bam! Bam! Bam! Bam!

Bam! Bam! Bam! Bam! Bam! Bam!

Bam! Bam! Bam! Bam! Bam! Bam!

Damn her.

A more bearish arctic fox he'd never known.

Grabbing a pair of sweats, he dragged them on, then stormed out of his bedroom, down the stairs to the front door.

He flung it open and glared at his sister and—great—her grizzly mate.

"It's about time." Isana shoved her way past him and as she moved by, he caught a strange scent of something foreign.

He whirled to follow and found himself shoved aside as Mason Worcester pushed by him with his arms full of bags.

Damn grizzly!

Scowling, Bryce turned to slam the door shut, but Mason shoulder checked him aside and stepped back out onto the front porch.

Bryce let out a low growl, went to slam the door shut *again*, only to have it flung back toward him by a massive grizzly paw in human form.

Bryce barely stopped the door from connecting with his face as Mason shoved by for the third time, this time carrying a strange box by the handle. "Now see here," Bryce snarled, turning to follow the grizzly down the hall. "What the hell is—"

He stumbled to a halt when he reached the door to his guest bedroom and finally realized what he'd been smelling. "Oh, hell, no!"

Don't miss the next adventure with the matchmaking cats of the goddesses. Grab your copy of A CATMAS TO REMEMBER today.

Thank you for reading

Please consider leaving a review on

your favorite book site.

If you would like to be notified of

Pepper's new releases, please sign up here:

www.peppermcgraw.com/newsletter

Join Pepper's reader's group on Facebook:

www.facebook.com/groups/theshenanigancrew

Other Books by Pepper

THE MURRYSVILLE COALITION

The Crazy Cheetah Lady

One Sad Kitty

A PAWSITIVELY PURRFECT MATCH

Catnapped

The Real McCat

Unbearably Cute

A Catmas to Remember

This Cat's for You

Santa Kitty

Hocus Purrcus

Tridents & Tails

Abra-Cat-Abra

Satan's Kitty

Valen-Cats

Vampurr Lovin'

A Beautiful Cat-ship

Grave Cattitude

THE SHENANIGANS SERIES

Shifter Shenanigans

Witchy Shenanigans

Full Moon Shenanigans

Hotel Shenanigans

Dragon Shenanigans

Undercover Shenanigans

Spooky Shenanigans

Holiday Shenanigans

Valentine Shenanigans

Lucky Shenanigans

STORIES OF THE VEIL

Guardians of the Veil

Astra

Glory

Luna

Zara

WICKED

No Rest for the Wicked

Wicked Is As Wicked Does

Anthologies & Collections

PAWSITIVELY PURRFECT TRILOGIES

THE CAT'S MEOW

Catnapped | The Real McCat | Unbearably Cute

HOLLY JOLLY PAWLIDAY

A Catmas to Remember | This Cat's for You | Santa Kitty

SHENANIGANS ANTHOLOGIES

CRAZED

Books 1-3

AMAZED

Books 4-6

HOLIDAZED

Books 7-10

SHENANIGANS

The Complete Collection

STORIES OF THE VEIL

THE UNVEILED

Astra | Glory

THE VEILED

Luna | Zara

WICKED DUET

WICKED

No Rest for the Wicked | Wicked Is As Wicked Does

About the Author

WWW.PEPPERMCGRAW.COM

PEPPER MCGRAW is a USA Today Bestselling Author of paranormal romance. Her life to date has sadly been paranormal-free, but she knows it's simply a matter of time before her fated mate finally appears. Until that glorious day arrives, she keeps herself busy writing (and reading) paranormal romances.

Pepper loves animals, especially cats, and spends her free time volunteering at local shelters and for Trap-Neuter-Release programs. She's had the supreme honor of winning occasional head butts and meows from the local ferals in her neighborhood and has even convinced a few to come inside and adopt her as their own.

BB bookbub.com/authors/pepper-mcgraw

f facebook.com/ShenanigansSeries

g goodreads.com/peppermcgraw

O instagram.com/peppermcgraw_author

d tiktok.com/@peppermcgraw

y twitter.com/peppermcgraw

www.ingramcontent.com/pod-product-compliance
Lightning Source LLC
Chambersburg PA
CBHW040534170726
48295CB00012B/465